SOMEWHERE OUTSIDE
OF SUNSET

KRISTI COPELAND

SOMEWHERE OUTSIDE

of Sunset

TEXAS SUMMER NIGHTS 1

ALSO BY KRISTI COPELAND

TEXAS SUMMER NIGHTS

Home in Paradise - Book 2

The Art of Loving - Book 3 (coming soon)

OTHER WORKS

Oakdale

For my husband:
my love, my king, my everything.

CONTENTS

1 COWBOY

ORANGE LIGHT in the shape of a gas pump flashed on the dash of the 1969 Camaro SS convertible. "Shit," Lanie Green cursed on the deserted road. The wind blew wisps of brown hair in her face as it flowed through the cabin of the convertible like a convection oven.

On the drive down back roads outside of Bowie, Texas, Lanie had gotten turned aroundwhile searchingfor the best area to capture the perfect sunrise photos. Split-rail fence lined both sides of the road and lulled Lanie into memories of the previous Christmas.

After a doctor's appointment, Lanie had arrived home from work earlier than usual and heard whimpers coming from the bedroom. She and Ron had talked about getting a puppy, so Lanie put her purse on the couch and bounced down the hall to the bedroom door. Shepictureda black lab with a red bow attached to her collar.

The last thing she'd expected to find was her boyfriend in bed—their bed—screwing the secretary from his office. Ron hadn't even noticed Lanie in the doorway until she barked his name.Needless to say, thatwas not the ideal way to end an engagement.

Lanie shook her head to escape the recollection and reached for her cell phone in the passenger seat. She wondered, for a split second, why the artistic picture of barbed wire didn't appear when she tapped the power button.

Lanie gasped. "Double shit." Her pulse increased and her face grew hot. She hadn't seen a human for miles; plenty of cows and lots of horses, but no humans. As she focused on the road ahead and maneuvered around a curve, a rancher came into view. "Thank you, God," Lanie whispered and exhaleda breath.

A man dressed in cowboy boots, jeans, a white T-shirt, and a cowboy hat sat on the tailgate of an old F-150. Tanned, muscled arms, flexed as he reached into the bed of the truck, picked up a guitar, and sat it across his lap. Under the truck, a Blue Healer rested in the shade.

"I have just been thrown into a country song," Lanie said to herself. "This cannot be happening." Warmth spread up her neck to her cheeks and accompanied a smirk. Lanie had always wanted to meet a real cowboy, not an impostor who put on a cowboy hat, boots, and a fake southern drawl.

When she'd met Ron at a country bar, he lured her into his world with a fake southern accent. He sure did look good when he dressed for a night out, but, as her mom always told her, looks could be deceiving. She was so right; the accent had disappeared the morning after their second date.

Lanie pulled the car onto the shoulder of the road, shifted into neutral, andput onthe emergency brake. She sent a silent prayer to the heavens asking for strength. Only God would be able to help her resist a true Texas cowboy.

The sound of the muscle car slowing caused Max Walker to raise his eyes; not one car had passed all day, let alone one that sounded like it had come straight off thedragway. He assumed some man from out of state had gotten lost and needed directions.

A red Camaro SS with white racing stripes pulled over and, to his surprise, a lady with brunette hair pulled into a bun sat in the driver's seat.

"Lordy, would you look at that," Maxsaid tohimself and took a drink from his thermos.

The lady, dressed for the Texas summer in short jean shorts, a white spaghetti strap tank-top, and over-sized dark sunglasses, walked around the front of the car. Max found it difficult to catch his breath.

Each step she took accentuated her thin but curvy frame and long legs thatseemed toreach all the way to heaven. The way the sun radiated behind her head, Max thought she must be an angel.

"Um, hi there, sir. Mister. Uh, I'm sorry to interrupt you," Lanie stammered.

A smile spread across Max's lips, his dimple almost covered by a closely groomed beard, as he did his best not to laugh; she was cute as a button, as his granny would say. "Darlin', I'm just taking a break with Sam here. What can I do forya?" The dog lifted his head at the sound of his name.

"Hi, Sam," Lanie addressed the Blue Healer from the road and smiled when he wagged his tail. "I hate to admit it, but I seem to be lost." Sunglasses covered her eyes and her hands rested on her hips. "My fuel light came on and I have no idea where the nearest gas station is. My phone is dead, so I can't google it. I haven't seen another two-legged in miles. Last time the—"

"Another what?" Max interrupted.

"Two-legged. Human. Non-animal." Lanie shook her head and frowned."Last time the low fuel light came on, I only had ten miles before the car stalled. These classics are a little more temperamental than newer cars. Pardon my French, Mr..." Lanie paused.

"Max, call me Max."

"Where the hell am I, Max?" Lanie stood on theopposite side of the ditch whereMax had been replacing fence posts before taking his break.

"Darlin', you're somewhere outside of Sunset."

"Perfect." Lanie pursed her lips and nodded. "I was searching for a sunrise."

"Pardon me?" Max tilted his head and squinted his eyes.

"I'm a wannabe photographer and my very favorite thing to capture is a unique and beautiful sunrise. I've been on these roads for hours trying to find the best area to get some great shots. Until I got turned around, that is."

"Well, sounds like you need a break too." Max nodded to the tailgate beside him as he sat the guitar in the bed of the pickup. "Take a load off. What's your name? You must be hotridin' around with the top down in that sweet ass car."

Lanie paused and looked left and right making note that there were no cars or other people in sight. *What if this guy is a serial killer? No one knows where I am,*she thought.*Ah, what the hell, you only live once, right?*She crossed the ditch with careful steps.

"It's ok, Darlin'. I don't bite." Max's crooked smile made Lanie's heart rate increase.

"My name is Lanie," she said. The steel of the tailgate practically sizzled when the back of her legs touched it. "Ouch!Wow, that's hot!" she cried out, jumpingaway.

"Sorry about that, Lanie. Here, sit on this." Maxgota towel from the bed of the truck, shook the hay off it, and laid it beside him.

The sound of this cowboy saying her name made her smile; she couldn't have kept a straight face if she tried.

Sam peeked his head out from under the truck and nudged Lanie's calf with his nose. She reached down to caress the soft fur on his head. "Sorry I scared you, boy."

After getting settled a few inches from Max, Lanie caught a hint of Stetson, her favorite cologne, and sighed.

"Ya like your tea sweet or unsweet?"

"Sweet, but..."

Max held out the thermos in his hand and Lanie shook her head. "Suit yourself." He shrugged and took a swig. A smirk formed as he pulled a plastic cup from the cooler behind Lanie, poured sweet tea from his thermos and held it in front of her.

Lanie accepted the cup with a nod and took a drink to distract herself from the pull she felt on her heart, not sure yet if it was attraction or panic. "Thank you, Max. I just love this weather and a cold cup of sweet tea is icing on the cake. We don't get this kind of heat in Michigan. Not very often, anyway."

She rested the cup on herthighand tilted her head back to absorb the warmth of the sun. Max stared at the smooth skin of Lanie's neck and chest, cursed under his breath, and shook the sexy thoughts from his mind.

"I thought you might be from out of town. Just you wait; it's not even summer yet. I bet by the first week of August you'll be seeking out any building that has air conditioning." Max chuckled. "What brings to you Texas, Miss Lanie?"

"Work. A fresh start. You know, the usual." A smile disguised a lengthy explanation.

Enamored with Lanie's perfectly straight teeth surrounded by full lips, Max pulled more information from his new friend. "Where's Mr. Lanie today? Did you leave him at home?" he asked with raised eyebrows; he hoped there wasn't a mister in her life.

"Eh," Lanie said dismissively and brought her gaze to Max. "I left his sorry ass back in Detroit. Long story. Fresh start, right?" She shook her head. "Where's Mrs. Max?"

"Eh." Max followed suit and shrugged. "She moved to Dallas. Long story." He winked making Lanie's heart race. "How long have you been in Texas? What made you choose this area?" Max removed his cowboy hat and ran a hand through a full head of dark hair.

Jesus, he's sexy, Lanie thought. Afraid she would stumble over her words like a teenage girl sitting next to a cute boy, she focused on keeping her voice steady.

"I accepted a job in Wichita Falls and moved to Bowie in February, so just about four months ago. My parents thought I was crazy for venturing out by myself, but I look at the move as an adventure.Nothing is keeping me up north, so I thought what the hell, I'm moving to Texas. I traded cars with my dad and started driving. What about you? Have you been here your whole life? Working on fences?" Lanie teased.

"Yep. Born and raised three miles east, as the crow flies. My grandparents own most of the farming land that's left in this area. My granddad passed away just after Christmas, broke Granny's heart. I'm doing what I can to help her, but the fence I'm fixing, here is mine. I talked Granny into splitting off 100 acres or so when I showed an interest in farming.

"A few families owned everything from DFW to Wichita Falls a hundred years ago, but most of it sold back to the state or broke into smaller plots. Mendin' fences keeps me busy.Or outtatrouble, as my dad says."

"Ah, that's no fun." Lanie nudged Max with her shoulder and swore she felt a spark.

"Speakin' of fun, that car is incredible; how many tickets have you gotten?" Max joked. "Just kidding. You said you traded cars with your dad. What did you trade for the Camaro?"

"Oh, I've luckily only gotten a couple tickets." Lanie giggled. "I had a four-wheel-drive Ford SUV. It was great in the snow, but I figured I wouldn't need it down here. Besides, my dad never drove the SS, so I convinced him it was a win-win. He restored it himself after retiring from racing small circle tracks."

"Well, darlin', it looks good on you," Max winked and Lanie looked away after a shy grin. "Your dad sounds like one cool dude."

"He is. I miss him and my mom but remind myself that I can always go home. Having a close relationship with my parents is very important to me. So many people take what they have for granted; I never want a life without my family."

Max grinned. "I think we have a lot in common, Miss Lanie. My dad pushes me to take more responsibility with the farm, but I keep putting him off. I try to make him proud, but I know I could do more."

Max gazed into Lanie's eyes, and a sense of calm ran through his body; this lady understood his every thought. He lifted his hand to reach for her but stopped before he made a fool of himself. He almost forgot that they had met only an hour ago; it felt like a year.

"I noticed your guitar. You play or just pretend?" Lanie found it easy to flirt with her new cowboy friend. The challenge was enough to provoke any man that seriously played and Lanie hoped that Max would play something for her.

"Oh, I don't pretend, Miss Lanie." He reached into the bed of the truck and pulled the guitar back into his lap. "I was justpracticin' my new favorite song. Tell me if you like it."

After strumming a few chords, Max cleared his throat and started singing.

Happy birthday to you
Happy birthday to you

Lanie threw her head back and let out a loud, genuine laugh. "Oh, my God. I was not expecting that. You have a great voice, Max. I would love to hear more."

Lanie caught herself getting too cozy and decided she had overstayed her welcome.

"Look, it's been really great talking with you, but I feel like I'm keeping you from your work. I should go. How do I get to the nearest gas station?"

Disappointed that Lanie had to leave but delighted she had stopped to chat with him, Max gave her directions. "Turn right at the end of this road; that's Denver. Follow it into Sunset, just two more miles, to the stoplight. Another right will take you to the interstate. There's a gas station there." Max lowered himself off the tailgate, tipped his hat, and said, "It's been a pleasure, Lanie." He held out his hand.

After a slight hesitation, Lanie grasped his hand and jumped off the tailgate. "You've saved my life. How can I ever repay you?" She turned to face Max and her knees weakened from his stare.

"Ah, darlin'. I've enjoyed my break and Sam seems to like you. Consider your debt paid."

BOXES OF PRE-MADE cake mix lined the shelves in the bakery aisle of Brookshire's, the grocery store in Bowie. Max pursed his lips and shook his head as he walked past the lemon, cherry chip, and German chocolate before he reached for the flour on the bottom shelf.

In his mind, a homemade cake always beat out box cake, especially when it was his granny's favorite. Even if it took him all night, Max would create the perfect birthday cake, just as his granddad had every year.

"Hey, stranger. Fancy meeting you here."

Max tilted his head at the familiar voice behind him; he couldn't believe his luck. An honest smile reached his eyes as he turned to face Lanie. "Howdy, darlin'. Nice to see you, again," Max drawled as he tipped his cowboy hat and reached to shake her hand.

Surprised by the shock when they touched, Max couldn't imagine anything that would cause static electricity in the middle of a grocery store aisle. "Uh, my directionswereok?"

A wave of dizziness washed overLanieand she steadied herself with her shopping cart. *Was that a spark?* she thought. The passion in Max's piercing blue eyes was unexpected and she tried to keep her voice steady. "Perfect. Made it back home without any problem, thank you, again." She pointed toward his cart. "Youmakinga cake?"

"Nope. I'm building a castle for the fire ants," Max replied without missing a beat. His smile faded when Lanie's browfurrowedand he shook his head. "Sorry. I try to be funny, but sometimes I only entertain myself. Granny's birthday is tomorrow, so I'm making her favorite cake. Need more flour."

"Ah, that explains why your new favorite song is 'Happy Birthday.' Well, Granny and I have something in common. My birthday is tomorrow too. Isn't that funny?" Lanie found herself starting to ramble. "Well, it was really great to see you again. I should let you get back to your day." She turned to walk away.

Max reached out and touched her forearm. "This might be a little forward, but..." He examined his dusty cowboy boots before meeting her gaze. "W-why don't you join us for cake tomorrow. If you don't have plans, I mean. For your birthday." Max didn't usually stammer, but this girl had him tripping over his own words.

"I don't even know your last name; you're almost a stranger. I'll have you know that I don't just go to stranger's houses on a whim." Lanie's grin was intoxicating.

"Oh, pardon me, ma'am. The name's Walker. Max Walker." With a slight bend at his waist, Max captured Lanie's gaze and winked.

Heatrose upto her neck and brought a natural pink to Lanie's cheeks. She murmured, "Green."

Confused, Max asked, "Green, what?"

Clearing her throat, Lanie regained control. "Green is my last name. Lanie Green. It's nice to meet you, again, Max Walker. Now that we've been formally introduced, I would love to join you for cake."

Proud of himself for remembering that cell phone reception is hit-and-miss near Granny's house, Max gave Lanie the land-line number along with directions to the farm.

On the drive back to the ranch, Max daydreamed about the way Lanie said his name. Not too harsh or shy, but strong and confident, like they'd known each other for a lifetime.

Although most would agree that Lanie Green was beautiful and sweet, Max saw something more than that in her eyes. Prior heartbreak had built a wall and Max had already made it his goal to break it down.

MAX'S electric blue eyes grew dark with passion before his mouth claimed Lanie's. Hungry kisses consumed them and Lanie's mind cleared of everything except Max. One of his hands reached into her hair, behind her neck, while the other wrapped around her waist. She found it difficult to catch her breath.

Lanie's wandering fingers caressed Max's back; smooth skin covered hard muscles that tensed under Lanie's touch. Her hands slid down his chest, moved to his torso, and landed on his waist. They took their time exploring each other's bodies for the first time.

When he pulled her even closer and let a groan escape, Lanie smiled under his kiss. She wrapped her arms around his shoulders, so they touched from their shoulders to their knees.

Grasping Lanie's hips, Max guided her two steps back before he lifted her off the floor, breaking the kiss to sink into lavender-scented sheets.

After he settled beside her, Max stared into Lanie's

eyes and ran his fingers from her cheek down her neck before tracing a line between her breasts. While his hand continued downher stomach, his lips followed the same path. Lanie arched her back, letting out a soft moan when his hand reached—

Lanie startled from a deep sleep with a gasp; she was shaking. Sweat soaked the sheets and herheart beatso fast that she had to force herself to breathe slower.

Heat radiated from the places on her body that Max touched in her dream. She could swear his skin remained hot under her fingers even though she was alone in her bed. Lanie could still sense where his lips landed hot on her breast.

If she looked in the mirror, she was sure that her flesh would be indented where his hands had gripped her hips and pulled her close.

"Jesus, that was hot." Lanie touched her lips, expecting to find them plump from passionate kisses. "Where did that come from? I don't even know Max. And I certainly don't need another man to disappoint me."

Max was right about the walls built around Lanie's heart and she promised herself, for the hundredth time, that she would keep them intact.

2 TOMORROW

"SARAH, it's no big deal, really. He's just a local guy who was nice enough to give me directions."

"But he's hot, right?" Lanie's best friend, Sarah, who was on the other end of the phone, could only guess based on her friend's airy voice and passive description. "You've always fantasized about dating a real cowboy. What's his name?"

Lanie's memory of Max's tanned skin and crooked smile brought a twinkle to her eye. "Yeah, Max is pretty cute. Not in a romance-novel, cover-model sort of way; he's not Fabio or anything. You know the sweaty, muscled guy with an unbuttoned shirt showing rippling muscles and a smoldering stare. He's cute in a Texas-cowboy way. He's tan and has lots of dark hair under his cowboy hat. And those eyes. Mmm."

"And he's a musician, to boot?" Sarah asked.

"I don't know if he's a musician. He just had a guitar..."

"But knew how to play it?"

"Well, he did strum his new favorite song for me," Lanie teased.

"Oh my God. See, I told ya. Which song?"

"'Happy Birthday.'"

Sarah's laughter came through the phone so loud that Lanie had to pull it away from her ear. She missed her friend and the way they would spend hours talking about boys and laughing until their cheeks and stomachs hurt.

"Why in the world is his favorite song 'Happy Birthday?' Maybe he isn't a musician. Maybe that's the only song he knows."

"Well, his grandmother's birthday is today too and Max invited me over to have cake with them."

"Whoa, whoa, whoa. Let me get this straight. You met a sexy cowboy, he's a musician, his grandma shares your birthday, and he invited you over for cake after talking with you for an hour? When's the wedding?"

"You're such a dork." Lanie huffed. "I barely know anything about him."

"One, he's a cowboy. Two, his family owns tons of land. Three, he has a truck and a dog. What else could you ask for?"

"Sarah, come on." Lanie giggled. "Besides, I'm not looking for a man, remember?"

"Girlfriend, stop kidding yourself. You've got it bad for Mr. Max. And good for you. Go have the time of your life without me down in Texas."

The girls laughed before Lanie promised to fill her friend in on all the details the next day, and they hung up.

With one last glance in the hallway mirror, Lanie

adjusted her necklace, smiled at herself, and tilted her head. "Hi, Max." She grabbed her keys off the hook on the wall and convinced herself that it would be a good day. "What's the worst that could happen?"

DUST FOLLOWED the Camaro down the long driveway to an old farmhouse. Lanie was sure that the paint was fresh, and windows were new, but the bones must be over one hundred years old.

Three steps led up to the wrap-around porch; a chair swing hung from rafters to the left of the front door. Max and an older version of him sat to the right in two rockers; Sam snoozed under a table between the men.

Max meandered down the steps as Lanie approached. She'd tried to compose herself before sliding out of the driver's seat; the sight of Max and the memory of the way he touched her in the dream was still fresh on her mind. She giggled, rolled her eyes at herself, and picked up the daisies from the passenger seat.

Max opened the car door and reached for Lanie's hand. A blush turned her cheeks pink and Lanie forced herself to look down at her sandals. A yellow sundress dotted with pink roses hugged her in all the right places. Sam begged for attention and pushed against Lanie's legs.

"Sam, stop that. You'll mess up Lanie's pretty dress." To Lanie, Max said, "You look beautiful, darlin'." He kissed her cheek.

The scent of Stetson cologne, her favorite, made Lanie shiver. She enjoyed the attention and wondered if it was typical southern hospitality or if Max seriously had an attraction toward her. She didn't want to back away and hurt his feelings, but she also didn't envision herself in a serious relationship anytime in the near future.

Max looked Lanie up and down; he took his time making note of the white sandals that supported her manicured pink toenails. Muscled calves led to the hem of Lanie's sundress and Max sighed. He wanted to see more; the shorts she wore the previous day allowed him to view smooth, tanned thighs.

"No." Max shook his head and corrected himself as his smile widened, a twinkle reached his electric blue eyes. "You look amazing. I'm so glad you decided to join us for cake. Come meet my dad." With one hand on the small of her back, Max directed Lanie to the house.

Sam led them to the porch steps where Fred Walker stood. Lanie thought Max's dad looked like Sam Elliott; kind eyes, the same electric blue as Max's, set between a black cowboy hat and a grin that peeked out from under a thick white mustache.

"Lanie Green, meet my dad, Fred Walker."

"Mr. Walker, it's a pleasure." Lanie reached out to shake his hand.

"The pleasure's all mine, Miss Green," Fred shook her hand and nodded his approval. "Nice strong grip. Someone taught you right," he said with a wink.

"Please, call me Lanie. My dad taught me not to shake hands like a girl."

Fred chuckled. "Smart man. Welcome, Lanie. My boy tells me you're new in town and share a special day with his grandmother."

The screen door opened and a short, plump older lady stepped over the threshold. Her white hair was tied in a bun at the nape of her neck and her flip-flops smacked her feet with every step. She wore an apron over a flower-printed calf-length dress and held a glass of tea in her hand.

"Boys, why are y'all hiding this pretty lady from me? Come in, come in. Lanie, is it? Well, aren't you just as cute as a button. You can call me Granny, just like everyone else does. I insist."

"Granny, these are for you. Happy birthday." Lanie held the daisies away from her chest. It felt a little weird to be so informal, but she rolled with it.

"Well, sweetheart, aren't these just lovely. Thank you. And happy birthday to you too, dear." With a change in focus, she turned to her grandson. "Max, what took you so long to invite this sweet young thing for cake?"

"Granny, we just met yesterday." Max glanced at Lanie with a smile and shrugged.

"Well, that's no excuse." With a wave of her hand, Granny dismissed the issue. "Are y'all ready for some cake? Lanie, I'll have you know that Max made my favorite Welsh desert, just like his granddad did every year on my birthday for over sixty years." Granny announced with her chin held high and pride in her voice. She then turned and led everyone toward the kitchen.

"That's so sweet of him. I don't think I've ever had a Welsh desert. What is it?"

"This cake is also the Queen's favorite cake. Granny swears she gave her the recipe in person, but..."

"She did, Lanie," Granny said over her shoulder.

"But that's a story for a different day. This cake is called the chocolate biscuit cake. The Royals use tea biscuits, but my granddad always made sugar cookies from scratch the night before. That's why I was in Brookshire's yesterday." The smile on Max's face warmed Lanie's heart. "After the cookies are broken into small pieces, you just mix the rest of the ingredients and chill it for a few hours. It's really just chocolate, butter, and sugar. Real healthy," Max scoffed.

"LANIE, dear, tell me about yourself. What brings you to Sunset, Texas? Max said you're from the north." Granny leaned back in her chair and laced her fingers over her stomach; Max had learned over the years that this means she was ready for a long conversation.

"Well, Granny, I'm from Michigan, an only child, and I love animals and fast cars."

Fred raised his eyebrows and glanced at Max.

"My parents still live in the house where I was raised, a suburb just north of Detroit called Royal Oak. I graduated four years ago with a Bachelor of Science in Land and Property Management with a minor in geology from Michigan State. After a short internship with a real estate market analysis company in Bloomfield Hills, they offered me a job.

"After some personal turmoil, I decided it was time for a change. An opportunity arose in Wichita Falls and I couldn't wait to move somewhere warm. I've always been drawn to Texas and the weather, compared to Michigan, was a massive appeal. So, here I am.

"Max tells me that you have lived on this land for generations. I daydream of owning enough land to raise horses and dogs. I wanted to be a veterinarian in my early college years, but the medical aspect made my stomach queasy."

"Oh, dear, your parents must be so proud. You're such a smart, lovely lady." Granny's compliment humbled Lanie, and she smiled in appreciation.

"How long have you been in Texas, Lanie?" Fred asked.

"Oh, I just moved at the beginning of February, so not even six months." Lanie sat back, enjoying the time spent with this friendly family. "I haven't had much time to explore yet. I can't wait to explore Dallas. I've been so busy studying the aspects of my job and taking the online training the firm requires that I've been pretty cooped up. I love visiting new places, though; I'm a photography buff on the side and love capturing images of beautiful things. Tell me, what should I see in the DFW area?"

"Well, dear, there's just too much to list. It sounds to me like you need a chauffeur. I know the perfect person for the job." With raised eyebrows, she turned to Max and cleared her throat, jumping at the chance to offer her grandson as a tour guide. "Son, I think y'all need to plan a day to take in some of the sights."

AS IF IT wasn't enough performing 'Happy Birthday,' Max felt compelled to play his new song. "I call this one 'Tomorrow.' Sam and I just wrote it yesterday." Max winked at Lanie as he strummed the guitar that sat on his knee.

> Tomorrow sounds like a better time
> Let's hang up our boots and find some-
>   where to unwind
> Why not call it a day and dive to the
>   tank
> If it weren't for Sam, last time I would
>   have sank
> Working in this sun is fryin' my mind
>
> Let's hang up our boots and find some-
>   where to unwind
> It's so hot; it's ninety-nine in the shade
> Sam, here really wants some lemonade
>   — don't ya boy?
> Who is that coming down the road so
>   slow?
> Guess I'll finish this fence tomorrow.

Lanie laughed and clapped along with Granny and Fred. Max had a beautiful, unique, steely voice and played the guitar like he was making love to it. Not that Lanie needed another reason to be attracted to Max.

"You all have been so kind. Thank you for the delicious cake and warm welcome to Texas, but I should be on my way. I've had a wonderful time."

The family joined Lanie on the porch to say their goodbyes.

"I feel I need to give you some advice, Miss Lanie." Fred's stare caught Lanie off guard. "If you're going to live in Texas, you need to catch on to some of the lingo before people start calling you a Yank." Fred smiled. "We never say 'you all.' For anything. Instead, it's y'all. Go ahead, Lanie, you try it."

Lanie pursed her lips, a little embarrassed. "Um, ok. Y'all have been so kind." She giggled.

Granny clapped her hands. "That's it, dear. Perfectly stated. It'll come natural in no time."

Lanie laughed and turned to walk down the steps. Max followed her and opened the door of the Camaro.

"So, um. I think Granny would be upset if I didn't offer to show you around Dallas. What do you say?" Max's eyes twinkled with humor.

"Oh, well if it's for Granny, how can I decline?" Lanie stood next to her car as they exchanged numbers. When they finished, she stood on her tiptoes and kissed Max on the cheek. He wrapped his arms around her waist and pulled her into a quick embrace.

MAX'S soft fingertips traced an invisible line from Lanie's ankle to her hip before his open hand glided over her behind. The pull of his grip brought their hips together and Lanie let out a gasp. As they faced one another on the lavender-scented bed, Lanie relished in Max's sensual kisses and reciprocated the desire for more.

Max's hand entwined in Lanie's hair and he pulled her head back so he had better access to her neck. After he rolled her onto her back, he planted hot kisses down her throat and then paused on her breasts for a long moment.

After a few heavy breaths, Lanie wrapped her fingers in Max's hair and encouraged him to come back to her lips. Their kisses turned hungry and transported the couple's passion to a new level.

Lanie's hands wandered over muscled shoulders, down Max's strong back, to a trim waist. When she couldn't take anymore, she gripped his ass and practically begged Max to...

Beep! Beep! Beep! Beep!

"What the?" Lanie found the alarm clock, smacked it, and swore. Heavy breaths and a racing heart accompanied her shaking hands.

"Again? What does this guy have over me? Damn these dreams..."

3 BAUER & BAUER

"LANIE, I think it's time you take on more responsibility." Lance Schmidt, Vice President of Bauer & Bauer, appeared in Lanie's office and dropped a stack of folders on her desk. Lance's uncle, Harry Bauer, was the founding member of the firm and the man that had offered Lanie the position as lead residential designer.

On Lanie's first day, Lance had called her into his office and gave her a practiced speech about expectations. Lanie's primary role was to act as the liaison between property owners and the finance department. In addition to Lanie's designs, she was responsible for the arrangement of meetings with landowners and any finalized details prior to close.

Even though her position's duties didn't typically require involvement in this realm of the business, Lance felt Lanie had the necessary people skills to enhance the product Bauer & Bauer sold. Not to mention, she was easy on the eyes; those tight skirts and heels made every man in the firm look twice. Many of the landowners they propositioned were older men that appreciated pretty women.

Her first major assignment was to assist the senior buyer, Calvin Fuller, as he convinced Earl Davis to sell three hundred acres to Bauer & Bauer. The small town of Sunset was long overdue for expansion. "It's about time that old stick in the mud shares the wealth, don't ya think?" Lance winked and added, "In the meantime, you will put together a modernized, economical design for the land."

In Sunset, huh...that's interesting. For the past few days, Lanie's every other thought revolved around Max and Sunset in some format. Maybe getting lost on that dirt road was meant to be. Set in the stars, as her mom used to say.

When Lanie pushed away the memory of Max touching her in her dreams, she wondered how close reality would match the fantasy. *Would his hands truly be that soft? Would his kisses be that gentle? Would they turn hungry so quickly?* Would she ever find out?

With a sigh, Lanie sat back in her chair and thought about the way Max's eyes shined just a little brighter when he gazed at her. It reminded her of the time she accidentally walked in on her mom about to kiss her dad. She'd had the same air of desire. Their obvious love for each other made their entire community jealous.

Why am I spending so much time daydreaming about this guy? Besides, it's too soon. I don't want a boyfriend yet. It could take months, years even, to meet the perfect eligible bachelor; there must be thousands of single men in the surrounding one-hundred-mile radius.

Why was I so attracted to the first hot cowboy that comes along? It's not like my biological clock is ticking or anything, I don't need to rush into a relationship.

He's probably not even interested; he hasn't called, has he? The longing in his eyes when he sang to me was unmistakable, though; he's interested. Lanie, damn it, get a grip. I have to find a way to focus on my work. Max will just have to wait.

The stack of folders seemed to mock her, so she picked up the first one; Lance left the Davis-Sunset file on top. The file contained minimum specifics about the desired land: owner information, acreage, terrain, surrounding farmland, and mineral deposits. After she drove through the small town, Lanie found it difficult to imagine a three-hundred-acre development in such a rural area.

Development software configured the details that Lanie typed in and she played around with the digital design. This addition could have a serious impact on Sunset. Good and bad.

Research of the area determined which specific additions could most positively affect the area. The current population of sunset was a mere six hundred and seventy-seven people. With the average U.S. household containing three point two three people, the population could increase by fifty percent if Lanie strategically designed this area with one-hundred affordable homes.

A park around the entirety of the lake would invite community members to leave their homes and get to know each other. *Ooh, a dog park*, Lanie thought, smiling to herself. Excitement, disguised as anxiety, caused Lanie's pulse to increase and her fingers seemed to type on their own.

In addition to the houses, Lanie added condos to the design. Her idea of a dog park, water park, skate park, and basketball court would be great areas for kids and young people to spend their free time. Four strip malls along the highway and eight restaurants behind them would bring in more money for the small town and create some well-paying jobs.

A gas station, an auto repair shop, and a veterinarian's office completed the roadside area while two churches were built within the housing area at a distance anyone could easily reach. Adults would have everything they needed within a mile of their home.

On the other hand, some small-town folks preferred their community remain just that— small with only the most basic necessities nearby. *But most people want to be near other people, amenities, and entertainment, no?* Lanie asked herself. Surely that was the case.

One perk of this position was being assigned an assistant. "Mary Lou?" she called out.

"Yes, ma'am?" A thin woman in her forties stood in front of Lanie's desk. Texans, or at least people in the south, had such good manners. It would take some time to get used to being called "ma'am."

"Would you please arrange a meeting with Earl Davis and Mr. Fuller? All their details are on the development questionnaire." Lanie handed Mary Lou the folder marked "Davis" and caught the scent of chocolate from a donut she'd eaten for breakfast. "Please schedule it in our calendars and send an email with details."

Unable to resist thinking about Max any longer now that her work progressed, Lanie took a minute to draft a text.

Lanie: *Hi, Max. Just wanted to say thank you, again, for Sunday. I had a wonderful time. The cake was delicious, the song was fantastic, and the company was inviting. Granny and your dad are wonderful people.*

THE MINUTE LANIE closed the dishwasher, a verse from "Toes" by Zac Brown Band played from her cell phone; she'd received a text message.

Max: *Sorry, Lanie, I didn't mean to be rude by not responding sooner, but I've had a long day in the sun. Do you have time for a quick chat?"*

A smile formed, stretching from ear to ear, on Lanie's face and butterflies filled her stomach. She didn't want to seem too eager, so she waited a full minute before she typed a nonchalant response.

Lanie: *Sure.*

The phone rang almost immediately. "Hey there."

"Hi, Max. Thanks, again, for Sunday. Has anyone ever told your dad he looks like Sam Elliott?"

"Yeah, he gets that a lot. I think it's the mustache. He swears he's a long-lost younger brother that must have been put up for adoption. Always the kidder, my dad. It was nice to have you over. Granny can't stop talking about you."

Lanie tilted her head and wondered why Granny... *Oh, she's playing matchmaker. Got it.*

"How's your week going?" Max's accent brought warmth to Lanie's face and a smile to her lips.

"Not bad, thanks for asking. Still adjusting to the new processes. You had a long day in the sun? You must be exhausted."

"Yeah." A chuckle came through the phone. "Working on that darned fence still. I feel much better after a quick shower though."

Mmm. A vision of Max's body from Lanie's dreams popped into her mind, so she closed her eyes and leaned back into the soft couch cushions before shaking her head to get rid of the image.

Before she had time to respond, Max continued. "Granny has asked me at least three times every day when I'm going to show you around Dallas. I meant to reach out last night but fell asleep in front of the TV. After I got your text, I thought I should call to see when, um, *if* you're available. Or interested. Maybe this weekend? What do you think?"

"You're asking because Granny has been pestering you?" Lanie asked, flirting.

Max caught on and flirted back. "Well, she can be pretty persistent."

"Well, because Granny obviously has an agenda, I suppose I should make her happy and agree to let you show me around."

Laughter rang like music in Lanie's ear. *Might as well have fun and explore DFW with a kind, handsome man. Whatever happens happens, but I highly doubt I will find true love, let alone in a tiny town called Sunset.*

"Saturday works for me; is that ok for you?" Lanie twirled a section of brunette hair between her fingers. "I wouldn't want to take you away from your fence."

"No worries, fence will be done by then. Saturday's perfect, darlin'. Should I pick you up after breakfast? Say ten?"

"That would be great."

"See you then. Bye, Lanie."

"Bye, Max."

A GLASS of amber liquid had Max's full attention. As he sat at the dining room table, opposite his dad, he tapped his fingers on the table. A furrowed brow accompanied pursed lips, "How did you do it, Dad? How did you convince Mom that you were the one for her?" When Max raised his eyes, his dad searched his face before he spoke.

"Son, I know you've had some heartache in the past, but you know by now that those relationships weren't meant to last. Those girls weren't right for you."

Fred's words were true and Max knew it. He didn't want to make the same mistakes and waste more precious time.

"When it's right, you'll know. It might even surprise the both of you."

"I'm already surprised, that's for sure. When was the last time you saw me the least bit interested in anyone? I'm so intrigued by Lanie; I want to know more. I want to know everything about her. I find myself thinking about ways to break down her walls. What's wrong with me; I just met the girl. I can tell she's been hurt, but haven't we all? I don't want to scare her off, is all."

"Just be yourself, Max. Take it slow; follow her lead. If it's right, you'll know it and she'll love you for you." With a final nod, Fred changed the subject. "How is that fence coming?"

"Another day or so and it'll be done. I'm sure you'll want me to start on mending the chicken coop, next." The Dos Equis went down smooth, almost too smooth.

"Nah, I'll have one of my men work on that. Look, Max, the fence can wait. We don't have cows in that area right now anyway. The next couple days are going to be scorchers. I think you to spend some time on your own ranch. You have a horse corral that you need to update, don't you?" A smirk stayed hidden under Fred's mustache.

Max smiled as he remembered the longing in Lanie's eyes when said she loves horses. "Yeah." He nodded.

4 DALLAS

WAAP WEATHER, Dallas, called for a high of ninety-two so Lanie put on a loose skirt and a white halter-top. She had worked on her tan so there was a contrast between the white of her top and her bronzed skin. Lanie strapped on her most comfortable sandals before she bounced down the steps toward Max's Mustang.

"Wow, you look fantastic." Max tried to control his wide smile but failed. A quick embrace and the scent of vanilla forced an exaggerated exhale.

Mission accomplished, Lanie thought and smiled. "Thank you." She curtsied before asking, "Where's your truck?"

"Did you think I would tour you around DFW in that old thing?" A crooked smile reached all the way to his eyes. "This here is my pride and joy. She's been pampered, though, so be nice to her."

"But of course." Lanie tilted her head toward her chauffeur. "What's her name?"

"What makes you think she has a name?"

"She's your pride and joy, been pampered, and you asked me to be nice. Max," Lanie caught his gaze, smiled, and lifted her chin. "What's her name?"

Max lowered his head and raised his eyes. "Her name is "Ellie", after Granny because she has always been the one constant woman in my life. The only one who loved me more than anything in the world."

"Aww," Lanie cooed. "You're sweet, Max Walker."

Pushed together by Granny's meddling, Max and Lanie headed to downtown Dallas for the day. Their first stop was Dealey Plaza, the historic location of President John F. Kennedy's assassination.

After they parked and walked toward the grassy knoll, Max gave Lanie a choice of two tours: a self-guided tour of The Sixth Floor Museum or a personal tour of the grounds from one of the many local guides.

Unsure of how she should answer, Lanie asked for Max's opinion.

"The museum is great. There's a ton of information so it will take a couple hours to walk through. If you want the real feel, the real story from people who have done tons of research and know the truth, we should do a personal tour. How much time do you have? That could make the decision easier."

Lanie answered with a shrug. "No curfew. No one's waiting up for me."

Max chuckled.

After considering her options, Lanie said, "You know, I'm not really big on museums, anyway, so let's just do a personal tour. Then we would have more time to explore other areas, right?"

The glow on Lanie's face and the fact that she wanted to experience as much as possible gave Max more than enough reason to be excited about spending the day with this beauty. He was confident that his companion would enjoy the sights and history of Dallas.

The couple had no problem finding an experienced guide on the sidewalk to show them around and explain that fateful day. Prepared with a binder full of public information and another with evidence and testimony that were never publicized, the guide began his practiced speech. The enlarged photos added a touch of realism to his words.

Halfway through the tour, Max glanced at Lanie and, recognizing the reason for her frown, put his arm around her shoulders.

Tears fell down her cheeks as she listened to the tour guide describe—in explicit detail—exactly what happened as the bullets rang out and 'struck the former president of the United States, causing his death. She leaned into Max's support, thankful for his silent understanding.

Lanie remembered one of the many documentaries about JFK's assassination she'd watched with her dad when she was a teenager. The image of Jackie Kennedy scrambling to the back of the limousine as she tried to pick up pieces of her husband never got easier to see.

After the tour, Max led Lanie to a bench in the middle of Dealy Plaza. "Come here. Let's sit for a while." From that angle, tourists could see the window where Oswald pulled the trigger, "X"'s in the middle of Elm St. that marked the location of the bullets that had struck JFK, the grassy knoll, and the exit to I-35, the route the motorcade took to the hospital.

"I can't believe people are actually laying down in the middle of Elm St. for a photo with an 'X.' What kind of sick people visit this city?" With a shake of her head, she dismissed the rhetorical question.

"Sorry to start off our day with such a depressing location, but in my eyes"—Max captured her gaze —"it's the most important."

Lanie nodded and sniffled. "It's ok and you're right. It is the most important." She pulled a fresh Kleenex from her purse, turned her head away from Max, and blew. "Thank you for bringing me here. I have a new appreciation for the life and works of JFK, as well as his assassination. There's nothing like experiencing a historical location like this in person."

After exhaling a deep breath, Lanie sat up straighter and smiled. "Ok, what's next?"

"You good?" Max questioned with knitted eyebrows.

Lanie closed her eyes as she nodded. "I'm good."

The strength in Max's grip as he helped her stand gave Lanie chills. That touch was different from when he put his arm around her; she had been distracted and that was a comfort. He didn't let go even after they began to walk.

When Max spoke, Lanie heard his muffled voice in the distance, but she couldn't make out the words. *Damn those butterflies.* She turned her head to hide a smile. Lanie fought the attraction to this tall, dark man, but she had a feeling she would lose.

Even if this isn't a long-term love affair, why not have

fun with this hot cowboy? He sure does look good in those jeans.

"Ok?" Max asked.

"Um, I'm sorry. I'm still reeling a little. Could you please repeat that?" Lanie tilted her head to get a better look at Max's profile. The chiseled jawline covered in a neat scruffy beard also had her reeling. A little.

With a squeeze of his hand, Max smiled. "Next place we're going is the Pioneer Plaza. Bronze statues of longhorns are a tribute to nineteenth-century cattle drives that passed through Dallas."

He was obviously in his element. Granny was right; Max was the perfect tour guide.

"After we're finished there, I want to show you a couple hidden gems before we make our way to the Stockyards."

SIXTEEN LONGHORNS SWAYED from left to right with each calm step they took down Exchange Avenue as they passed in front of the livestock exchange building.

Their horns led the way during the twice-daily cattle drive through the infamous Stockyards of Fort Worth, or "Cowtown," as the locals called it. The cattle drive allowed visitors to get an up-close-and-personal view of the majestic creatures.

From their viewpoint on the sidewalk, Max explained a little about the animals. "These boys are chosen specifically for this job. Only the best-mannered steers are asked to be included in The Herd. This is the twentieth anniversary of the Cowtown cattle drive; these boys here are making history.

"The Texas Longhorn breed is represented by showcasing the drastic differences in color and horn patterns, size, age, and personalities. You'll notice not one longhorn in this little herd is the same as another. It's quite an honor, not to mention pretty prestigious, for one of your steers to be invited to join the team."

"They're just beautiful. Breathtaking. And so...big." Lanie's wide eyes made Max chuckle. With each step the cattle took, the distance between man and animal decreased. Anxiety quickened Lanie's pulse.

"Yeah, they're pretty big." Max smirked.

"Johnny!" a woman standing on the other side of a large family shrieked. Max moved so fast that Lanie didn't realize he had left her side until he returned with a four-year-old boy in his arms.

"Max?" Not able to grasp what had almost happened, Lanie's gaze jumped from Max, who had his hands on his hips and pursed lips, to a woman who was blubbering while her son cried in her arms, to the unaffected cattle, and then back to Max.

"Ma'am, that's why the cowboys ask that everyone stay on the sidewalk. These animals are the best-natured, but..." The woman and her snotty-faced four-year-old started to walk away as Max was mid-sentence so he stopped his speech and huffed. "Not even a thank you. Wow, some people." Max shook his head. His demeanor softened as he moved close and stared into Lanie's eyes. "Darlin', are you ok?"

The gentle touch of his fingers on her face took

her breath away; she nodded and fought to find her voice, "I have no idea what just happened." Her gaze followed the lucky four-year-old through the crowd.

A deep breath calmed Max enough to tell Lanie that he just saved a boy from being trampled. "What I tried to tell the mother is these cattle are the best of the best, but they're still animals. They don't mean to hurt anyone, but anything can happen. That could have been real ugly, darlin'."

After glancing at the dispersed crowd, Max led Lanie to an alley behind the livestock exchange building. Cowboys surrounded the cattle pens that housed the longhorns. Most of them either tipped their hat or said "hello" to Max as he and Lanie passed.

A brindle longhorn with a W brand on his hip snorted at Max when he reached between the bars of the gate to touch the cow's face. "You ok, boy?" The cow grunted and leaned into Max's hand. "Whew, that was a close call, Rascal. Good job staying calm; didn't miss a beat, did ya? Proud of you."

Lanie leaned against the metal bars of the enclosure and observed the cowboy. Max's shoulders relaxed and he rested his forearms on the gate while the longhorn nuzzled his hands. With his head leaned toward the cow, as if he was listening to a whisper, Max chuckled. "Yeah, I know. I miss you too."

"Max?" Lanie didn't want to interrupt but found it fascinating the way this animal responded to him. "Is Rascal yours?"

Dust rose from the dry ground as Max turned to face Lanie. He smiled and nodded. "This big guy was my buddy for the first three years of his life. He followed me around like a puppy dog. When he was born, his momma, Gracie, didn't know how to care for him so I gave him a bottle six times a day until he could fend for himself. Gracie is still on the land, but we haven't bred her since."

With compassion in her eyes, Lanie tilted her head and grinned. "That's so sad. And so sweet. And so happy. What a fantastic friend you are."

"What else could I do? Poor fella was so lonely. Became my best friend in seconds."

"HMM. These are a little—how can I describe them? Mushy? What are they called again?" As Lanie chewed the appetizer, her eyebrows pulled closer together.

"They're called Calf Fries. It's a Stockyards delicacy. It's an acquired taste." With a chuckle, Max popped another one into his mouth.

Riscky's Steakhouse was owned by one of Fred Walker's best friends and when any family member came to the area, they were guaranteed a superb dining experience. Each of their steaks was award-winning, but their filet mignon was Riscky's pride and joy.

"Are you sure it's not too much if I order the filet? I can pay my own way..."

"Darlin', stop it, now. You're gonna hurt my pride." Max winked. "I insist. Order whatever your little heart desires. It's not too much."

Once Max had ordered for them both and the waitress walked back to the kitchen, Max gazed into

Lanie's eyes. The seriousness of his stare caused her to blush and look away. "I'm sorry, Lanie, you're just so damned pretty. I can hardly take my eyes off you. Where did you get those emerald-green eyes? It's almost as if they can see right through me. I'm hypnotized." With a tilt of his head, Max smiled his crooked smile and Lanie laughed.

"My grandma on my mom's side," she admitted. "People used to stop her in the middle of the mall just to look at her. They would find any excuse to start up a conversation. She was absolutely stunning." Lanie shook her head, focused on her fork, and pursed her lips. "I miss her every day. She passed away almost a year ago." When she raised her eyes to meet Max's, a single tear slipped down her cheek.

"I'm sorry, darlin'." Max reached across the table and squeezed Lanie's hand.

"Thanks." With a brush of her forefinger, the tear disappeared. "I saw where you got your electric blue eyes. Your dad is a very handsome older man. I bet your mom couldn't take her eyes off him."

The smile that lit up Max's face faded and his attention turned to the napkin in his lap. "Talk about missing someone every day." The touch of Lanie's fingers on his hand gave Max a reason to talk about his mother. "She died in a car accident when I was twelve."

Lanie gasped and Max looked up at her. "I'm so sorry, Max. That must have been just horrible for you."

"Thanks. It was." He paused. "Granny became my second mom and helped raise me while my dad and granddad kept the business running. God, I look back, now and feel sorry for all the crap I put her through. She is one tough bird, let me tell ya. For more years than not, I tried so hard to remember only the good parts of my mom; I think I may have turned her into some sort of fantasy. Now, I wonder if my memories are real or if I made them up."

The light returned to Max's face and Lanie let out the breath she didn't realize she was holding. "Even if you made them up, the memories make you smile, right?"

Max nodded. "You're so smart, Lanie Green."

"I HATE TO ADMIT THIS, but I haven't had this much fun in weeks. Months, maybe." As they strolled from the Stockyards shops back to the car, Max expressed how Lanie had brought out a suppressed version of himself.

"I haven't had this kind of connection to anyone in ages." He stopped in the middle of the sidewalk and turned to face Lanie. Her hand felt natural in his. "It's not just me, is it? Don't you sense something special here?"

Lanie wasn't accustomed to a man being so expressive with his feelings. She liked it. A lot. But she remained skeptical. Even though she felt a spark from the moment they met, it was just too soon for something real. *Wasn't it?* This must just be a crush on the first cute Texas guy that paid her any notice.

"Max..." she began but her shoulders sank as she exhaled and looked away.

One step closer put Max merely inches from the beautiful lady that captivated him. His fingers touched her chin and guided her eyes to meet his. Max tilted his head and whispered, "Lanie."

Her name on his lips brought warmth to Lanie's cheeks. She lost herself in Max's eyes. "Yes?"

Another half-step brought Max close enough to inhale the scent of Lanie's vanilla perfume. While he stared into her eyes, Max moved his hand under her hair, to the back of her neck, and lowered his head toward hers. He paused just long enough to give Lanie a chance to move away, before he closed the space, wrapped his other arm around her waist, and touched his lips to hers.

Lanie grasped Max's arms so her knees wouldn't buckle as waves of dizziness passed through her. The short, innocent kiss was even more exciting than those of her dreams. *Shit,* she thought, *I'm in so much trouble.*

"I have to see you tomorrow," Max spoke before Lanie had a chance to open her eyes. Once she could focus on his face, he smiled. "Please let me take you on a different kind of adventure."

5 THE TANK

THE UNMISTAKABLE ROAR of Lanie's Camaro brought a smirk to Max's lips. He loved that this girl owned such a kick-ass car. His attraction to Lanie increased with every minute he spent in her presence.

Max secured a cooler, a basket, and a box in the back of his side-by-side and turned to lean against the fender so he could observe Lanie. As the top of the convertible raised, he watched her remove her pony-tail-holder and shake her hair into place.

Brown cowboy boots with pink highlights proceeded Lanie out of the car. As she stood, the pink sundress fell into place around her thighs. Max let an audible "oh man" escape, thankful that Lanie couldn't hear him. *This is going to be a great night.*

"Hey, you made it," Max glanced at his watch and thought, right on time. He sauntered over to Lanie and opened his arms. "Wow, you look incredible."

Electric blue eyes almost hidden under a black cowboy hat mesmerized Lanie. "Thanks, you look pretty great, yourself." With a smile, she fell into Max's warm embrace and took in the citrus and sage fragrance of her favorite cologne. She hoped that Max couldn't hear the deep exhale as her smile widened.

Lanie backed away and glanced to the ground in an attempt to quash this overwhelming attraction; it's not the right time in her life for a man. How could she be sure he wouldn't break her heart? Or that she wouldn't break his?

Max took her hand and led her to the side-by-side, Sam bounded beside them. "Your chariot awaits, my lady." After Lanie fastened her seat belt and Sam nestled between the cooler and the box in the back, Max started the engine and began the tour of his land.

Multiple paths led from the house to specific areas of the property; Max took the one to the right. A brief wooded area opened to a barn and expansive pasture with several clusters of Texas Longhorns; a group of a dozen or so gathered by the fence.

"Max," Lanie said loud enough to be heard over the UTV, "this is incredible. All these animals are yours?"

"Yup." Max stopped the vehicle. "This is just some of the herd. The others are separated into two other pastures. We rotate them through five pastures every week, so the vegetation has a chance to grow." He observed his guest and smiled at her wide eyes and open mouth as she surveyed the view before her.

"Granny sold me this land, but it was more of a verbal agreement. Because of all kinds of legalese and confusing contracts, she couldn't outright sell it to me. We both have a strong desire to make sure that Sunset isn't overdeveloped and between the two of us, we are determined to keep this land natural. Anyway, our property is all joined and the cows roam most of it. These guys are a few of the four-year-old steers."

Lanie studied each of the cows for a moment before moving her attention to the next. "They're gorgeous. They all look so different. Do they all have names?"

"Of course, they do." Max raised his arm and pointed at each of them, "Sampson, Willy, Fredrick, after my dad, Joel, Adam, Reginald, Earl, after my granddad, Charles, Henry..." When he finished introductions, Max said, "I hope you got all that. There will be a test at the end of the night."

A genuine laugh from Lanie caused Max to nod and revel in his ability to amuse the beautiful lady by his side.

"Rascal was part of this here group. Luckily, the big guy won't be coming home. They only allow the most docile bulls to walk the Stockyards. Rascal proved that he has what it takes to stay calm under pressure. His momma, Gracie, is part of the group of gals. We keep them in a separate pasture. We'll have to go to the Rodeo next time we're at the Stockyards. You'll love it. A couple of Granny's Brahma bulls are the most difficult to ride."

"OH, my, Max. This view is amazing. Just beautiful. From this elevation, you must be able to see for miles." After Lanie stepped out of the side-by-side, she wandered around the area and detailed each aspect that would make the perfect photograph.

"The pond at the bottom of the hill surrounded by longhorns, that old oak tree to the right, the barn with a split-rail fence, the woods over there," Lanie paused to glance back at her guide. "I could spend an entire day out here taking pictures."

Her frown concerned Max. "What's wrong, darlin'? Are you ok?" Sam sat beside Max's boot and looked at Lanie as if he waited for her to answer.

Lanie pursed her lips as she re-examined the landscape. "I didn't bring my camera."

With a chuckle, Max put his arm around her shoulders and whispered in her ear, "There's plenty of time for that. Don't you worry your pretty little head." He swore Lanie shivered under his touch before she lowered her eyes to study her boots.

"Here." A blanket appeared in Max's arms. "Take this over there so we can sit and relax."

The red-and-black plaid blanket floated to the ground and covered long grass next to a live oak; *the perfect spot,* Lanie thought. She took the basket from Max as he set a cooler next to the tree. A box sat beside the cooler and Lanie tilted her head and wondered what Max had up his sleeve.

The couple settled on the blanket and Sam turned in a circle before he curled into a fluffy ball at one corner.

"Sam is the best," Lanie said. "I miss having animals, but it wouldn't be fair to adopt a friend when I'm never home."

"What's your favorite critter? One you could keep in the house," Max asked.

Besides a cowboy? Lanie thought, giggling. "I love dogs, but cats are more my style. Easy. No need to walk them twice a day, no poo to step in if I miss a spot in the backyard." Taking in Max's grin, Lanie continued. "Once I'm settled on a nice piece of land, I plan on having tons of animals."

Enamored with the surroundings, Lanie gazed at the vista, stretched out her legs, and leaned back on her elbows. "Dogs, cats, horses, chickens."

"I love that you're an animal lover. What else do you love? Besides beautiful skies and exploring new cities." Max found it difficult to focus on anything other than Lanie. His heart raced from the closeness of their bodies.

"Hmm, lots of things." A shiver ran up Lanie's arm as she turned to look at Max. Such a strong attraction was unusual in such a short time; she focused on her voice and tried not to ramble.

"I love the smell of race gas, of fresh-baked bread, Stetson cologne..." Her voice trailed off as Max moved closer.

"What's your favorite thing to do when it's raining and you have to stay inside?"

Max's intense gaze and low voice caused Lanie to hesitate. She smiled and teased, "who says you have to stay inside when it's raining? I love swimming in the rain; in a big, deserted lake after everyone else covers their boats and runs inside because they're afraid they might melt."

Desperate to learn more about Max, Lanie

returned the question. "What about you? What do you love?"

Max turned on his hip and leaned on his elbow to face Lanie. "I love the smell of horses and leather, fresh-baked apple pie, Granny's hugs." A strand of hair fell across Lanie's cheek and Max reached to move it over her shoulder. "A gorgeous brunette."

Lanie stared into Max's eyes as they grew dark with passion. He moved closer and caressed her cheek with his thumb. When his lips touched hers, a zap startled them both.

"Did you feel that?" he asked and smiled, his lips almost touching hers.

With wide eyes, Lanie whispered, "We're creating our own electricity."

Even though Lanie's attraction to this cowboy had been stronger than expected, she still had things to work out in her head before moving into something serious. It probably wouldn't last, anyway, and she didn't want to hurt anyone.

Lanie glanced over Max's shoulder at the mysterious box next to the blanket. She longed to let this man ravish her, but she knew that the timing wasn't right. *Take it slow. There's no rush,* she reminded herself.

"The suspense is killing you, isn't it?" Max asked, raising an eyebrow.

Lanie sat up straighter and peered around Max to get a better look at the box. "Like a dagger sticking in my heart."

Max sighed, "All right, darlin', I've teased you long enough." He placed a quick kiss on her lips before turning to pick up the box. When he placed it in front of Lanie, she lifted her hands, ready to dig into the surprise.

In the box, Max had packed a Canon camera with a wide-angle lens, a tripod, and wrapped two additional lenses in bubble wrap. From years of watching the sunset in this spot, he understood that conditions were perfect for a fantastic spread of colors. Lanie would surely be eager to take pictures.

Once she opened the box, Lanie sat back and tilted her head. "Max..." she murmured, then forced her voice to be louder, "How do you already know me so well?"

Max touched her face, held her stare, and brushed his lips across hers.

When he backed away, Lanie exhaled and gave an honest smile. "Thank you."

"Go." Max nudged her away. "Take the perfect picture for me. I want something new to hang above my mantle."

Motivated to get the perfect shot, Lanie stood and bounced around to different areas. Sam followed her and wagged his tail as if he sensed her excitement. As she crouched in the long grass for one picture, then bent at the hip to capture Sam in the foreground for another, Max sat back and grinned; he enjoyed the chance to study Lanie in her element.

MAX FILLED two plastic glasses with wine and handed one to Lanie. "I hope you like this. It's from a local winery called Marker Cellars. It's advertised as 'Texas

Sunset in a glass,' so I thought it would be perfect for tonight."

They clinked their glasses in a toast and an appreciative smile reached Lanie's lips. "To Texas sunsets."

"And new friends," Max added before he took a sip.

"Mmm. This is delicious." Lanie tilted her head. "Roses? And strawberry." She took another sip and nodded. "Fantastic, Max. Perfect. What's it called?"

"Texas Bluestem Blush."

"Well, cowboy, you just added another item to my love list," Lanie beamed. "Hold, please." She handed the glass to Max, grabbed the camera, and stood. "Need to capture these incredible colors."

Max almost forgot they were here for the sunset. He held both glasses and watched Lanie as she moved to the spot she had decided earlier would create the best picture. She set up the tripod and started to shoot. Clouds streaked the space above the tank with the most vibrant colors Lanie had ever seen; the pictures would certainly turn out to be beautiful.

When she came back to the blanket, she posed the wine glasses together at the edge of the blanket and positioned herself low to the ground.

"Beautiful," Max whispered as she leaned close to get the shot. He noticed her grin as she tried to focus on the view.

As the couple sat in silence while the sun sank below the horizon, Lanie couldn't help but compare her experience with Max to previous men she had dated. The last time someone took the time to get to know her in this way was... Well, never.

Ron hadn't bothered to ask about her favorite color, the things she loved, or even her middle name. The two guys she dated before Ron had been only first dates. One talked about his work the entire date, which was an instant turn-off, and the other, after absolutely no spark, asked if she kissed on the first date.

And to think that only a few months ago, in my mind, cowboys were just someone hot to look at who rode horses and bulls at the Rodeo. Who knew I would happen to meet one that is actually interested in who I am, where I came from, and what interests me? He's such a gentleman, sweet, and thoughtful.

Max proved to Lanie that there truly are men out there that pay attention to how she's feeling. He noticed if she was comfortable or sad and was concerned if she frowned. *The icing on the cake is that he's gorgeous. That cowboy hat is so sexy. The way he looks at me is intoxicating, my god, those eyes. I feel like I'm in junior high and practically forget my words.*

"Penny for your thoughts?"

Max startled Lanie out of her trance and she chuckled. "Just a penny?" she teased, attempting to avoid the question.

"Mmm-hmm." Max waited.

Dammit. "Um, I think you're kinda cute." Lanie blushed as she glanced at the hunk on the blanket next to her.

"I think you're kinda cute too." Max leaned forward and kissed the tip of Lanie's nose before he stood and walked to the side-by-side. He turned on a lantern and sat it beside the oak tree; light illuminated the space on the blanket.

A guitar sat in Max's lap and he began to play. The lightest touch of the strings produced the most beautiful sounds. When Max's voice added to the melody, Lanie thought she would literally melt.

> You have a way of making me forget
> Your pretty smile makes me sigh
> I love the way you blush when I stare
> > too long into
> Those emerald eyes
> I want to know everything about you,
> > darlin'
> What's your favorite color, your middle
> > name?
> Do you have a tattoo? Do you feel the
> > heat from this flame?
> You're so free, so alive
> So beautiful, independent, and strong
> I just had to write a song about
> Those emerald eyes
> What am I thinking? I just met you
> But I want more time; I've gotta make
> > you mine
> How did you end up in my dreams?
> Please tell me the stars are aligned.
> Darlin' you're so free, so alive
> So beautiful, independent, and strong
> I just had to write a song about
> Those emerald eyes
> Those emerald eyes

I want to kiss you every time I
    stare into
Those emerald eyes

Lanie leaned forward, not able to take her emerald eyes off her cowboy. Her heart raced and she became dizzy, but nothing was going to keep her from kissing the gorgeous man that had written a song about her.

The guitar kept Lanie's body from touching Max's as she placed the first kiss on his smiling lips. He moved it out of the way as fast as he could and shifted Lanie to sit in his lap.

Lanie's hands cupped Max's face and she took the time to look into his eyes before she pressed her lips to his.

Max wrapped one arm around Lanie's waist and pulled her closer, as he slid the other hand under her hair. He tilted her head before he brushed his lips across hers. When he opened her mouth with his, deepening the kiss, Lanie pressed herself against him and moaned.

Under his shirt, Lanie felt Max's muscles flex as he lifted her off his lap and shifted her to the blanket. She leaned back, guiding him so their mouths didn't part.

The slight of her body under his reminded him to be gentle.

As he moved his hand from her hip up her side and over her breast, Lanie breathed, "Oh, god," and arched into the palm of his hand. Lanie's sighs in response to Max's touch encouraged him to go further than he originally intended. Their hunger grew deeper with each caress and Max forced himself to hold back his passion.

"Lanie. Max's breath between hot kisses on her neck made her shiver. "Darlin'..." He backed away just enough so he could look into her eyes.

"Max, we need to slow down. I'm sorry, I got carried away."

"Don't apologize. I'm the one who got carried away. You're just so damn sexy I can hardly look at you without wanting to..." With a sigh, his voice trailed off into a gentle kiss. Max helped Lanie sit up but refused to break their touch.

"Listen." He brushed her hair over her shoulder and smiled at her pink cheeks. "As much as I would love to make love to you, I need to know that we're on the same page. I don't have casual sex—not that I'm insinuating that you do—but when I do make love to you, there will only be you in my life."

Lanie lifted her chin, so she could look directly into Max's intense gaze and brought her hand to his cheek. "As much as I would love to make love to you, I need to know that both of our hearts are ready for something serious. I don't have casual sex either."

Max's face lit up with relief and he cupped Lanie's face to give her another taste of his enthusiasm. He invited her to sit between his knees and lean back against his chest. The sun fell below the horizon and only streaks of dark orange lingered.

He's right, Lanie thought. *I've been telling myself that it's too soon. Making love can wait, but, God, I hope not for long. This cowboy is so freaking hot. I need to be honest with myself and be sure that my heart is fully committed before moving forward.*

"You know, until yesterday, I kind of felt like I was just here for a special work assignment. I didn't really feel like Texas was home." Lanie admitted as she turned to gauge Max's reaction.

His intense stare was enough for Lanie to sense the walls around her heart start to crumble. "I wonder if I wasn't letting myself get too attached in case I decided to go back?"

"And now?" Max stared into her eyes as he held his breath.

Unable to look away, Lanie sighed, "I never want to leave." She lingered as Max's face inched toward hers. The anticipation of what would come next filled her with desire.

Max touched her cheek and exhaled her name before his lips covered hers, again.

At that moment, she started to fall.

6 STRANGERS

COLORED pencil shavings littered Lanie's desk beside the drawing plans for the new Fruitland Estates development. The leather chair creaked as she kicked off her heels and leaned back to take a break. She rubbed her tired eyes with the heels of her hands and visions of Max came to mind.

He'd told her that when he made love to her, she would be the only one in his life. He was so confident that what they had would turn into a relationship; Lanie wasn't quite as sure. Although she'd enjoyed the time she had spent with Max and the way he devoured her with his eyes made her squirm.

The memory of her most recent dream made her quiver with anticipation. Max had bent his knees to reach under her dress, ran his hands along her thighs and over her behind. When he realized she was wearing a thong, he groaned, "Good God," and then kissed her neck. His mouth moved over hers and he kissed her with a new hunger.

With the dress gathered on his forearms, he continued to caress her skin as he moved his hands up her sides. When his palms reached her bare breasts and lingered there, he gasped, "Oh, Lanie."

Max lifted the thin cloth over Lanie's head and backed away to gaze at her perfect body. "You're so beautiful. How did I get so lucky?"

"This is looking really good, Lanie."

Surprised, Lanie opened her eyes, exhaled, and her smile fell. She hadn't noticed anyone had entered her office until Lance Schmidt spoke.

He leaned over the plans and examined each detail. "A dog park; I love it. That's a splendid idea. Very 'big city.' Listen, I hear that the meeting with Calvin and the Davis family is set for next Monday. Why don't you take your drawings along and show them what you plan to create? That's not a typical strategy for Bauer & Bauer, but it may put things into perspective; let the seller know that a plan is already in place and it's going to be great for their community to grow. Younger families in the area could really make the city of Sunset prosperous."

"Sure, Lance." Lanie regained her composure and focused on her work. "They'll be ready by then. There's no reason I can't share them." She shifted in her chair, picked up a green pencil, and added a few trees to the park.

Her mind wandered back to Sunday when Max had told her he was determined to fight the overpopulation of Sunset and she struggled to take a deep breath. How could she plan a development that would surely add over two hundred bodies to an area that hadn't been touched in decades? Was she a fraud?

This is my job, she reminded herself. This was the sole reason she'd shifted her entire life from Michigan to Texas. She had earned a degree in land and property management for the unique purpose of designing subdivisions.

Lanie dreamed of living life on a chunk of land with tons of animals; was it hypocritical of her to want to build beautiful places for those who didn't share her dream? What would Max think when she told him what her job entails? That Bauer & Bauer had hired her to provoke his biggest fear?

A goat sound came from her phone and made her smile. The text notification was a silly choice that Sarah talked Lanie into before she'd left for Texas.

Max: *I might be a few minutes late. Just finishing up a project. Shouldn't be later than 7:15. Is that ok?*

Lanie: *You bet. I'm finishing up a project myself. See you soon.*

THE CLOCK on the microwave read 6:42. Perfect timing, Lanie thought. She set the timer for thirty minutes and took off the Bluebonnets-and-Texas flag apron that Max bought for her in the Stockyards. She was proud of herself that she had been able to keep it clean.

After a quick shower, Lanie blow-dried her hair, spritzed her skin with her go-to vanilla scent, and pulled a comfortable pale green sundress over her head.

She loved how this specific dress hugged her top half and flowed to her knees. It was also the dress she'd worn in her dream, so she decided on a thong and no bra. She felt a little naughty and a lot sexy, like Baby in Dirty Dancing.

I carried a watermelon? Lanie thought to herself and giggled at the quote from the movie.

As she stepped into the kitchen, the timer sounded at the same time as the doorbell. She tapped 'stop' as she walked past the microwave and exhaled the breath she held. As she opened the front door, the sight of Max standing in her doorway made the butterflies return to her stomach. *Oh, man. I'm in trouble.*

"Wow, you look fantastic." Max greeted Lanie with a kiss on the cheek and a bouquet of summer flowers. "As always." His cowboy hat covered his eyes as he allowed himself an extended examination of the beautiful lady that stood before him.

"Thank you. I'm so glad you're here." Lanie twisted her hips so her skirt sashayed around her and took the flowers. "Come in, please."

"Is that lasagna?" Max lifted his gaze; his mouth watered, and he licked his lips in anticipation of dinner. "It smells so good! I'm famished." His stomach growled, but he couldn't tell if he was hungrier for the food or for Lanie. A crooked smile appeared. *Both*, he thought.

"It is. You said you like Italian food; this is my specialty," Lanie said over her shoulder as she reached for a vase in the cabinet. "Make yourself comfortable. This will just take a minute."

Max sat at the dining table as Lanie floated around the kitchen. He studied her bare thighs as she stretched to reach the cabinet above the refrigerator. "I like Italian food, but don't get that confused with pizza. I don't do pizza."

After Lanie took the pre-plated salads from the refrigerator and placed them on the table, she put her hands on her hips and tilted her head. "Wait. What? Did you just say you don't like pizza? Who doesn't like pizza?"

Max raised his hand and chuckled.

With a laugh, Lanie turned and continued to prepare plates of lasagna and garlic toast. All day long, Max had watched the clock while working as fast as he could; he looked forward to this time with Lanie more than he wanted to admit.

"I WAS ENGAGED. Until a few months before I moved here. It hasn't been that long and I've been struggling to get it out of my mind. Still trying to not blame myself." Lanie knew this conversation had to happen eventually. If she and Max were going to have any sort of relationship, she had to be absolutely up front with him; it couldn't wait any longer.

"Go on." Caring blue eyes reflected her emotion and Max reached across the table for her hand.

Lanie enjoyed the comforting touch; it relaxed her and she knew the man sitting across the table had a kind heart. "I walked in on him having sex with his secretary. Total cliché, I know. I have heard plenty of stories from girls about a cheating boyfriend, but nothing compares to actually seeing them in the act. I was devastated. I found out it had been going on the entire length of our relationship." Lanie shook her head and let out a halfhearted laugh. "This was the man I agreed to spend the rest of my life with. What the hell kind of judgment do I have in people?"

"I'm so sorry you had to go through that, Lanie. Obviously, you must know that he didn't deserve you, right?" A squeeze accompanied his statement.

"Yeah, I guess." Lanie sighed and her eyebrows knitted together. "I just feel so stupid for believing all the lies. It all made so much sense once the details came out, though." With a shake of her head, she dismissed the visual. "Enough about that. I'm so over it. Tell me about your love life. What happened with your last girlfriend?"

"She wanted more than I could give. She wanted to be a city girl and live in a brand-new house in a suburb between Dallas and Fort Worth. We met after a Cowboys game. I think she just wanted to be with the visual of a cowboy. She never wanted to see me without my Stetson and refused to spend any time on the ranch." Max shrugged. "Didn't last long, but it still hurt to know that I let myself care for someone that only wanted the idea of me. Like I'm not good enough as just a person."

"I'm sorry you had to go through that." Lanie offered a sincere smile. "I've known people like that and decided pretty quickly not to waste my time in their presence. Fake is not my thing."

Electric blue eyes twinkled and gave Lanie chills. She stood with Max's hand still in hers. "Come here. I have to show you my favorite place in this house."

Beyond the screen door, Lanie led Max to the deck dotted with comfortable lawn furniture. She sat on the seat made for two and patted the space beside her.

With a grin, Max sat and held her hand. "You know, I grill a mean steak if you ever want to break in that Weber."

"That what?" Lanie shook her head and frowned.

"The charcoal grill." Max nodded to the pristine grill that sat on the edge of a patio made of brick pavers. "You ever use it?"

"No." Lanie laughed. "My dad bought it and insisted that I put it in the moving truck. I don't know how to grill." She glanced at Max. "I love a good steak. Filet, though. I'm a little high-maintenance when it comes to food."

"Got it. Filet." Max nodded and made a mental note. "I can see why this is your favorite spot. The sunset tonight is beautiful. You sit out here often?"

Lanie nodded and asked a question that had been on her mind. "Max, this may be a difficult subject, but can I ask what happened to your mom?"

A smile spread across his face at the memory of his mother, "My mom was the best. Just the best." Through closed eyes, Max remembered life with his first best friend.

After a chuckle and a sigh, he focused on Lanie.

"She made the best pies, award-winning pies. Each time I walked through the door, she had something baking in the oven. She loved animals, cats mostly," Max winked at Lanie and she smiled. "And horses. She used to breed Texas Thoroughbreds and trained them before finding them loving homes.

"My dad used to call her the critter communicator; she just had a sixth sense. She was patient and kind and loving and beautiful." The smile on Max's face faded as the last memory of his mother came to mind. "A drunk driver hit her head-on when I was twelve. She died instantly."

A small gasp escaped Lanie's throat and she whispered, "Max. I'm so sorry." She held his hand and gave a gentle squeeze; she wanted Max to understand that she was there for him.

"It sucked. Still does." A tear leaked from Max's eye. "I think about her every day. Still talk to her. I think she listens." After a pause, he continued, "My dad lost it. Was inconsolable. Until recently, we couldn't even discuss my mom. He stayed sad, and mad, and distant. Granny took over the parenting duties for a while; that's why she's so special to me. Dad worked out his anger and Granny loved me through the hardest part of my mom being gone."

Lanie's eyes filled with tears as she witnessed Max's emotions change.

"My dad loved her so much. Back then, I didn't know what it meant to love a woman as your wife. I can't begin to imagine going through that kind of loss; it was bad enough for me, but I was so young and it's totally different. Now, if God forbid, anything happened to you, I'd want to remember the happy times we spent together. If I met the right person, maybe I'd remarry and be happy again. Not like my dad who held in so much resentment."

Lanie didn't know what to say; he just spoke as if they were married. She offered an honest smile and reveled in the love he expressed for her. She held her questions about what he meant exactly so the moment wouldn't be ruined. He was telling her he loved her in his own way. Even though she refused to let herself fall, she wanted to ride out the possibility of something real.

"She would've loved you. Would've just adored you. You're a lot like her. She loved to travel, and explore new areas, and witness beautiful scenery and sunsets. That spot by the big oak tree was her favorite place on the property. Sometimes, when I need to feel her presence, I grab a couple beers and go to the top of that hill to watch the sunset disappear."

"Just like that Luke Combs song," Lanie added, giving his hand a compassionate squeeze.

"Yeah, exactly. I could go on for hours about my mom. She was perfect in my eyes." Max smiled as he lifted Lanie's hand and kissed the back of it before he stood up. "I'll be right back. Don't move."

Confused, she hoped she hadn't struck a nerve. She stayed put as Max requested.

When Max returned with his guitar in hand, a smile lit up Lanie's face. She repositioned herself so they faced each other on the couch. Max sat down, lowered his gaze to his hands, and picked at the strings. His voice started out soft and when he lifted his eyes and sang directly to Lanie, heat ran up her chest to her cheeks.

> Who is that pulling up my drive?
> The sight of her makes me come alive
> I just met her, I barely know this girl
> How is it that she has already become
>   my world?
> Hell, we're practically strangers
> Who is this beautiful stranger?
> The sound of her voice is like angels
>   singing in my ear
> Her scent makes me come alive
> Who is this beautiful stranger?
> I want to spend all my time with her
> I want to explore new places and feel
>   her heartbeat
> Will she let me break down her walls?
> She must know I won't hurt her
> I want to spend all my time with you,
>   Lanie
> Til we're no longer strangers

When Max finished the last chord, Lanie wiped a tear from her cheek and leaned in to place a soft kiss on his lips.

"Max, I'm sorry I'm emotional; that sincerely moved me. I'm just blown away at how talented you are; that was incredible and so beautiful." Lanie touched his face and kissed him again. "Thank you." She took a deep breath as Max sat the guitar on a chair and moved closer.

Lanie placed her legs over Max's as he caressed her back and stared into her eyes. "I'm smitten with you, darlin'. I think you can see that." He placed a light kiss on her lips without taking his eyes off her; his hand slid up her leg and under the edge of her dress. "I can't get you out of my mind. It's difficult to get any real work done because I find myself daydreaming about you."

Lanie giggled because, although she understood where he was coming from, she wasn't quite ready to admit it. They inched closer to each other with increased anticipation. Lanie's pulse quickened and Max's eyes turned dark. Once their lips touched, a shock made them smile and their passion increased. Max's mouth claimed Lanie's and he breathed his love into her.

Without breaking their connection, Lanie straddled Max's lap offering him easier access to explore her curves. His hands moved further under her dress and when he discovered she was wearing a thong, he groaned with desire. It was all he could do to not carry Lanie into her bedroom and ravage her.

Max wrapped her hair around his fingers and guided her head back so he could kiss her neck. His teeth gently grazed the delicate skin and his excitement grew as Lanie's breathing quickened.

"Max".

The sound of his name on Lanie's lips was almost too much for Max to bear; he couldn't get enough.

Max pulled away and concentrated on slowing the pace. "Lanie..." He leaned his forehead against hers and closed his eyes. "I want to be with you, I'm sure you can feel that." Encouraged by a nod from Lanie, Max adjusted himself so he could capture Lanie's full attention and continued. "What I don't want is for what we have to be hindered by lust."

Lanie tilted her head and absorbed the meaning of Max's words. "I've never had a man be so utterly sincere with me." She smirked. "It's quite refreshing, honestly. I agree, Max. I've been trying to suppress the attraction I have for you, but you make it so incredibly difficult." She kissed him with desire, confirming her statement, before she continued.

"You're so different from anyone I've ever met and I love it. I love how you look at me, how you talk to me, how you kiss me," Lanie accepted the brief brush of his lips on hers with a smile. "I love how you are a thousand percent open with me. I feel like I could tell you anything, good or bad, and you would tell me that you'll be here, no matter what."

"There's no place else I would rather be than with you." Max guided Lanie to stand and seized her gaze. He never wanted to let her out of his sight. "Let's get more comfortable."

Lanie followed him into the living room and when he started to sit on the couch, she tugged his hand and backed down the hallway to her bedroom. A smile radiated from Lanie's face; Max's crooked smile mirrored hers.

"I HAVEN'T TOLD you that you have been in my dreams, too." Sweat covered the skin on Max's chest and she pressed her body into him; she couldn't get close enough. Lanie ran her hand through the short hair in his chest and down to his six-pack abs. "The first day we met, I had the sexiest dream about you. I woke up shaking."

"And you're still shaking," Max winked before he kissed Lanie's swollen lips; she wrapped her arms around his neck to make sure he didn't stop.

"Things you did to me just now were a hundred times better than in my dreams."

His electric blue eyes twinkled with passion and he turned Lanie on her back, desperate to express again how deeply he cared for her. "Ah, darlin, we're just getting started."

7 BROKEN

STARTLED BY THE DOORBELL, Lanie set the garlic salt on the counter. *Who could that be?* She didn't know many people in Texas, let alone anyone well enough that would stop by unannounced.

A smile spread across her lips as she pictured Max on her front porch. Her pace quickened. She ran her fingers through her hair and hoped she still looked presentable.

Through the curtain that covered the window in the door, the unmistakable silhouette of a cowboy hat made her heart leap. *I thought he was taller.*

"Hey, baby." The sound of Ron's voice made Lanie's stomach churn; heat rose up to her neck as she balled her fists. Furious, she forced her ex-fiancé three steps back as she stormed out the door to a muggy, ninety-degree porch.

Fragrant roses almost touched Lanie as Ron pushed them toward her. "Wow, you look --"

"What the hell are you doing here?" Lanie interrupted.

"What? I...I thought..." Ron stammered. "Why aren't you happy to see me? You should be relieved that I followed you here. Just because you ran away when you thought it was over doesn't mean I don't still want to be with you."

He squinted and shook his head. "Ungrateful," he muttered under his breath.

"When I ran away? You seriously think I ran away? From you? I moved here for a job opportunity. The fact that I found you in bed with your secretary just made the decision easier. I seem to remember having this discussion before. What do you want?"

"Well, baby, I want you. I want you to leave this godforsaken town and come home. It's ok that you took some time away; I forgive you. Come back to Michigan. I'll still marry you."

A loud laugh escaped Lanie's lips and she threw her head back, unable to prevent the wide smile that spread across her face. Impossible to hold in the laughter, she clasped her hands against her chest and almost bounced in place.

With outstretched arms, Ron moved closer. Unable to stand the thought of his touch, she backed away. "Wow, I forgot how egotistical you are. Thanks for the reminder. And thanks for the laugh. Hilarious! You forgive me. You've lost your mind.... Wait, how did you find me?" Lanie tilted her head for a moment, then shook the question away. "You know what, never mind. I don't care. You need to leave."

"I'm not leaving without you, babe. We're going

back to Michigan to start our life together. You owe it to me to come home and marry me." Ron reached for her again, but this time Lanie slapped him across the face.

"Leave. Now." Lanie pursed her lips and struggled to remain calm. Ron frowned and didn't move, so she closed her eyes and repeated the last word loud enough for her neighbor to turn his head. "Now!"

LANIE'S SMILE said it all. Another man in a cowboy hat handed her roses and she leaned her head back to laugh; she bounced with elation. Through the windshield of the Mustang, Max witnessed the woman he loved accept a bouquet of roses from another man. Happily.

As Max sped away, he questioned Lanie's integrity. *We had an agreement; neither of us wanted to see other people. I certainly don't. Didn't. What if I hadn't stopped by for a drive-by kiss? Would she have kept seeing him behind my back? So much for surprises. How could I have been so naive? Why does every woman I care about want to be with someone else? What am I doing wrong?*

The Mustang's tires squealed as Max took the corner too fast. Pressing down hard on the gas pedal, Max welcomed the adrenalin that came from the speed of his sports car. He turned up the radio and let the bass of Metallica's "Enter Sandman" vibrate through his body. Max hadn't played this song in months; the beat matched his anger.

Once Max pulled into his driveway, the dust

settled, and another song started before he let go of the wheel. "Damn it," he huffed; the image of Lanie's smiling face as she entertained another cowboy refused to leave his mind.

A rolled up, enlarged photograph that Lanie had taken of the sunset on the hill sat in the passenger seat. Max wanted to surprise Lanie with how beautiful the colors turned out and share his excitement with her. *Obviously, she had other plans.*

Sam greeted Max at the front door. The dog sensed his master's negative energy at once. A whine caused Max to focus on Sam's unusual demeanor. "Hey, buddy. What's wrong?" Max sat the photograph of the on the counter before leaning over to stroke Sam's fur. All Sam needed was to understand that his owner was ok; he wagged his tail and licked Max's hand.

"SARAH, you won't believe what just happened." After calling Max and leaving a brief message, Lanie called her best friend in Michigan to explain the bizarre day she'd had. "He tried to hug me. Seriously. What the hell was he thinking? That I would be so happy to see my cheating ex-fiancé I would just forget everything that happened and fly home with him?"

"Wow, girl. I can't believe he showed up on your front porch! The nerve."

"You know, seeing him made me rethink the entire situation. I can't believe I blamed myself for his cheating. How could that have possibly been my fault? I'm finally confident in how I feel about him; I am totally and completely over Ron. Honestly, I have been for months, I just didn't realize it until now."

Lanie pulled a bottle of wine from the fridge and poured herself a glass. "I have to admit, I've been trying to talk myself out of having feelings for Max, telling myself that it was too soon. Seeing Ron on my porch made me wish Max had been standing by my side. I want to be with him."

An unintentional gasp surprised Lanie and she almost spilled her wine. "Oh, my God. I just said that didn't I?"

"Yes, you did. I can't wait to meet the man that has you swooning. You're head over heels, aren't you? I'm so happy for you, Lanie."

"In the short time we've known each other, we have spent some real quality time together. He's opened up about intimate life stories and details of his past and so have I. I am absolutely comfortable with him and there are no red flags. Well, except that he hates pizza. I mean, seriously, who doesn't like pizza?"

Sarah laughed on the other end of the phone. "No one. Your man is a weirdo so..." Sarah paused. "You know I have to ask. Have you...you know?"

"You know I don't kiss and tell." Lanie couldn't hide the smile in her voice.

"And? How was it? Spill, girl!" Sarah read her friend better than anyone.

"Better than my dreams."

AFTER THE FOURTH unanswered phone call and seventh text in two days, Lanie began to worry that something bad had happened to Max. *Why would he ignore my calls? Something must be wrong.*

"Granny? I'm really sorry to interrupt your evening and I don't mean to concern you, but..." With a shaky voice, Lanie asked, "Is Max okay? He hasn't returned my calls and I'm starting to worry about him."

"Oh, dear, no need to worry, he's fine."

Relief spread through Lanie's entire body; she sat on the couch and sighed. "Thank God."

"To be honest, though, he has been awfully grumpy the past couple of days, not his normal jovial self, and I've actually been a bit concerned myself. Did something happen between the two of you?"

"We had dinner Wednesday, talked, watched the sunset, and had just a beautiful evening. I have no idea why he won't respond to me." Embarrassed that she reached out to her date's grandmother, Lanie tried to end the call. "Again, I'm sorry for bothering you. He's ok. That's all that matters. Thank you for your time."

"Lanie, you're not bothering me one bit. Please don't hang up, dear. I think you should know that yesterday morning, he was all smiles and his face shone brighter than the sun. He's never in a bad mood when he greets me in the mornings, but he's never been that happy. Ever. He was humming an upbeat tune and almost walking on air.

"I knew y'all spent time together the night before. It was quite obvious that he had fallen in love and I'm over the moon for him. And you, dear. My Max is a good man. Then, this morning things were completely different. He had a frown, was shaking his head and muttering to himself. I asked what was wrong and all he said was that he couldn't believe he could be so stupid."

"GRACIE, WHAT SHOULD I DO?" Max asked the longhorn that stood still as he brushed her. One of the other girls snorted to get his attention. "Ok, Bessie, you're next. Promise." He grinned. "All you girls want is attention." Sam's bark made Max chuckle. "You're just as bad. Thanks for making me feel better, guys. I knew I could count on you."

Even, consistent strokes of the brush on the heifer's back calmed Max as he thought about the past few days with Lanie and how his love for her grew in such a short amount of time.

Their time in Dallas and the Stockyards, Lanie had been up for anything; he loved an adventurous date and longed to share his life with a woman that wouldn't shy away from new things. Her appreciation of the sunset, the need to photograph and forever capture the essence of all things beautiful, and love of all critters, big and small, hit home; she reminded Max of his mother.

Lanie touched Max in emotional and physical ways that he had never experienced before. Even if he tried, it would have been impossible to hide the love he felt for her.

And those emerald eyes. Hell, I even wrote songs about her; I haven't written in a year.

"I love her, Gracie. I don't want to let her go, but she obviously already found another man. I'm not into sharing my women and I fell for it when she said she wanted our hearts to be on the same page before we made love. Boy, was I a fool. I thought only men used those lines to get someone in bed. I guess she got what she wanted, didn't she? I'm such a schmuck. I hate how much my heart hurts. I can't catch my breath, I can't smile, I can't erase her from my mind. How could I be so naïve? Argh, my life sounds like a country song, doesn't it?"

Gracie rubbed her head against Max's hip.

"Gee, thanks, girl. Well." He sighed. "Now what? This love business fell through pretty damn quick, didn't it? I really don't want to take over the business side of the farm, but I don't want to disappoint Dad. For the last couple weeks, I thought maybe I could make a life with Lanie and settle. I could let go of my dreams for her, couldn't I? For a normal happy life, like Dad did?

"Should I just say, 'screw it, I'm done with women' and be a lonely hermit here with Granny and Dad, or should I focus on my singing, and chase the dream that Dad never supported?" Gracie turned her head as if she contemplated the question.

Max repeated the two choices again but this time the words came out slower with more significance. "Should I stay here, lonely forever, or chase my dreams?"

The last three words made him smile.

"That's it. I guess I better brush up on my stage presence and singing voice if I'm going to send CDs to producers in Nashville. If they decide I have what it takes and give me a chance, I'll be ready. Thanks for your advice, Gracie."

After a quick shower, Max ran by Granny's to apologize for his funk, kissed her on the cheek, and sped down the driveway. Dust followed the hum of the Mustang.

THE RACK RESEMBLED a ranch home with stairs that led to a wrap-around porch. One of Lanie's co-workers mentioned that the pub on Mason Street had live music on Friday nights, so she decided to do something different to escape her sorrows.

Dressed in her favorite black dress and pumps, Lanie wanted to feel pretty without attracting attention. Although every time she didn't want attention, some poor unsuspecting guy would hit on her, and she had to put on her nice face to turn him down. She just wanted to unwind and release some negative energy. Nothing more.

When she walked through the door, a familiar voice rang through the speakers and gave her pause. She tilted her head to be sure she was right.

> Her scent still lingers on my skin
> How can I erase the feel of her lips on
> mine?

Lanie stood straighter, pushed a five-dollar bill into the bouncer's hand, and rushed through the double doors into the bar area. The instant that the image of Max on stage registered in her mind, she stopped dead in her tracks.

> I just wanted her to let me in
> I prayed to find a love that would last
> I thought this was really it

A black Stetson covered Max's face, but Lanie knew it was him as he strummed the most heartbreaking chords she had ever heard. He sat on a stool hunched over his guitar that rested on his leg. His voice cracked as he sang the next line.

> Will the whiskey make me forget?

She couldn't help but wonder what had happened that made this gorgeous man so sad. Lanie listened to the lyrics and realized the song was about her.

> She was my princess; I wanted to give
>   her all I have
> Is that too much to ask
> I've never felt so much passion, so much
>   love
> Now my heart is broken, laying on the
>   floor
> She smashed it
> Will the whiskey do the trick?
> I need to drown her memory before she
>   ruins me

Why would she suck me in just to be
    with another
How could I be so naïve,
How could I let myself fall
Will the whiskey be enough?
Will the whiskey work at all?

Tears streamed down Lanie's face as she watched Max. What have I done? Lanie had only recently accepted that the feelings she had been so desperate to avoid were those of love.

At the end of the song, the crowd erupted with applause and whistles, but Max simply stood and walked off the stage.

"Max!" Lanie hurried through the crowded room and tossed "excuse me" and "pardon me" over her shoulder when she bumped into a table or a chair. "Max!"

Thankful that he stopped, Lanie touched his shoulder frantic to understand what had happened.

Max sighed and lowered his head before he turned to face her. His pursed lips and squinted, eyes emitted sadness and pain. He waited five whole seconds before he asked "Why, Lanie?"

She gasped, shook her head, and breathed, "Max."

Max turned and walked away, his guitar in his arms.

Lanie tried to follow, but the bouncer held her back. "Max! Max!" Lanie cried, unable to reach him.

8 COME BACK

EYES STILL PUFFY from a night of tossing, turning, and tears, Lanie cringed as she looked in the mirror. Her hair had tangled like a rat's nest and her nose red from blowing. The tank-top she slept in had twisted around her waist, making her walk sideways.

She must have sent a dozen texts and left at least six voicemails on Max's cell phone last night. At first, she explained how she was confused by his reaction to seeing her, then she cried an embarrassing apology for something she must have done wrong, still unsure of exactly what that was.

By three am, Lanie was furious. She couldn't understand why he was mad at her and texted to ask why he couldn't just be open with her and tell her what she did to deserve such treatment.

"Shit!" Lanie turned off the burner and moved the pan of burned bacon off the heat. Thoughts of Max demanded her focus. This kind of reaction wasn't like her at all; she never begged for a man to explain why he didn't want to be with her.

In the past, if someone gave her the cold shoulder, she just walked away and chalked it up to avoiding a future break-up. Then again, she never adored anyone like she did this cowboy.

"Adored?" Lanie thought out loud. "I haven't ever said that about anyone. I'm so screwed."

Lanie sat at the table with her chin in her hand and pushed her eggs from one side of the plate to the other. Without the bacon, it just wasn't breakfast. Her shoulders slumped as memories of the last three days played like a movie in her mind. *What went wrong?*

Wednesday night, Lanie had gotten home from work, cooked lasagna —*does he not like lasagna? That's ridiculous,* she thought. They sat on the back porch and —*did I react wrong when he talked about his mom? No. That can't be it.*

Did I not respond well to his song? It was beautiful. It was about me, for God's sake. He opened his heart to me. I didn't tell him how I'm feeling. Is that why he's upset? "Ugh, what do I do, now?" Coffee cooled in the cup in front of her, so Lanie stood to pour a warm-up, then leaned against the counter and remembered the best part of the night.

"The way he touched me, kissed me, made love to me, I thought he would never leave my side. I thought I had met the man of my dreams." Creamer swirled in her mug and turned the black liquid to a chocolate hue; Lanie stared into the coffee as if it were a crystal ball. A single tear ran down her cheek and she wiped it away before others had a chance to follow.

"Maybe he really is what I pictured a cowboy to be —a womanizer who just wanted a quick romp in the hay. Wham bam, thank you, ma'am." With eyebrows that formed a 'V,' Lanie shook her head. "Nope. No way. Not Max. Damn it," she whispered under her breath and sighed.

I don't get it. He won't return my calls; he won't talk to me. Obviously, I must have done something that he can't forgive me for. If he can't confront me about it, then I guess it's his loss, right? If he doesn't want me, then I guess I will have to talk myself out of wanting him.

"Suck it up, Buttercup," Lanie told herself. "Just forget about him and move on. It's a beautiful day; let's go enjoy it." As if she held a conversation with someone other than herself, she admitted, *but I love him. Shit.*

STRIPES RAN along the driver's side of the Camaro as Lanie drove south on Highway 287 toward Alvord. She had looked up the Marker Cellars Family Winery and decided to check it out for herself. The wine that Max brought to the picnic on the hill had impressed Lanie and she wondered what it would be like to do a real wine tasting.

During the twenty-minute drive, Lanie did her best to convince herself that Max must not want to be with her; it would be best for them both if she just got over it. Over him.

The highway was unusually busy for a Saturday

afternoon and when a white F-150 passed in the fast lane, Lanie swore it was Max that sat in the driver's seat. She had to shake her head to get rid of the visual.

Downtown Alvord was about the same size as Sunset; a church, a gas station, a grocery store, and some homes lined the main street. Lanie stopped at the railroad crossing and a tall, slender man in a cowboy hat crossed in front of her car. She had to do a double take to make sure that it wasn't Max. *He's everywhere.*

After some twists and turns, Lanie was remembering the day she'd gotten lost and pulled over to ask a rancher—a hot rancher and his dog—for directions, when her GPS announced that she had arrived. A modern sign inside a rustic frame welcomed Lanie to the winery.

All the stories she had heard about wineries throughout Napa Valley, France, and Tuscany had not prepared her for the downhome, friendly environment at Marker Cellars. She'd almost expected a snooty sommelier to scoff at her because she was inexperienced with wine.

To the contrary, a very pleasant man introduced himself, seated her, and asked what type of wine she preferred. Lanie shook her head. "I really don't know. I'm pretty new at this."

The man offered a warm smile and asked if she liked sweet or dry.

"I've had the Texas sunset in a glass and I liked that one a lot."

The man convinced Lanie to do a tasting of the

white wines and nodded. "Very well. I'll be right back." She leaned back in her chair and enjoyed the view of horses as they grazed in the pasture. This is just beautiful. Exactly what I needed, today—an escape from reality.

Something licked Lanie's hand and fur filled her palm; a black-and-white dog nuzzled her as if he knew she needed a friend. "Well, hello," Lanie smiled and she realized it was the first time she had smiled all day. Animals had a way of bringing out the best in people. *I miss Sam. Dammit, girl, keep it together.*

The owners of the winery visited with each of the parties as if they were life-long friends. "How is everything?" A woman approached and presented a genuine smile.

"Oh, just fine, thank you. You have a beautiful place here. I'm really enjoying the atmosphere," Lanie responded.

"Thank you so much. Is this your first time here? You don't look familiar."

Lanie nodded. "First time to any winery, actually."

"Really? Well, welcome. I'm so glad you're here. Where are you from? What brings you to Marker Cellars?" The woman sat at the table with Lanie as if she were sincerely interested in her response.

As she scratched the dog behind his ears, Lanie grinned. "I just moved to Bowie from Michigan a few months ago. Long story, but I tried a bottle of your Texas sunset in a glass on a date last weekend, loved it, and thought I would check out where it came from. Honestly, I'm just here to get away from the real world for a little while."

"Well, it's a pleasure to meet you. I'm delighted that you loved our wine and this is the perfect place to escape. My name is Becky; my husband over there is Mark. We own the winery; please let us know if you need anything." The dog followed as Becky checked on other patrons.

A young lady had been seated at the table next to Lanie and they exchanged smiles. After the first three tastings, Lanie's entire body began to relax and she became more open.

She enjoyed the scents and flavors of the different wines, along with the descriptions of how they came to fruition; she had no idea there was so much more to wine than just white and red.

Becky introduced herself to the lady at the next table and turned to Lanie. "Excuse me, I'm sorry, I didn't catch your name."

"Lanie." *Did I just slur my own name? Ooh, this stuff is good.*

"Lanie, this here is Julia. What a strange coincidence, she just moved from Michigan to Paradise, about a half-hour from here." Almost like Granny, Becky played matchmaker. *Bless her heart, she's trying to help me make friends.*

An hour later, Becky's mission, accomplished, Julia had moved to sit at Lanie's table, so they could talk. They discussed their lives in Michigan versus Texas, the companies they work for, and stories of recent loves lost. Even though Lanie thought better of it, she expressed her desire to reconnect with Max.

They both tried most of the white wines, chatted with some of the regulars, and learned the history of the area. Through the laughter, they agreed that a day that started out as confusing and almost depressing had turned a sharp corner to engaging and enter- taining.

"Hey, Lanie." Julia tilted her head and blonde locks fell across her cheek. "I'm having a July Fourth party for my team in Paradise. If you and your man are back together by then, please join me. Maybe I will have someone to spend time with by then too." Julia touched Lanie on the arm and nodded with raised eyebrows.

Lanie returned the nod and smiled. "Ok. Even if we're not, I would love to join you."

Before they left, Julia and Lanie exchanged numbers and promised to keep in touch. Lanie couldn't remember a recent day when she had more fun. Well, unless she included the days with Max.

ON THE DRIVE HOME, Lanie couldn't stop her mind from running through the last few days, again. This time, she picked out different aspects of each day and gasped when one specific detail came to mind.

"Oh, no. No, no, no," Lanie remembered how Ron showed up on her front porch the day after she and Max had a magical, lovely evening.

When Ron pushed flowers toward Lanie, she'd laughed in his face. Was it possible that Max had seen them together and gotten the wrong idea? What if he watched her laugh but left before she'd slapped Ron?

Could he possibly think that she was involved with someone else the day after they made love?

Desperate to get to the bottom of this once and for all, Lanie pulled into her driveway, hurried through the side door, and sat her keys, purse, and three bottles of wine on the counter. Her hand shook, making the buttons difficult to press, as she dialed Granny's number.

After three rings, the lines connected. "I know what happened, Granny." Instantly sober, Lanie started to explain before anyone spoke on the other end of the line.

"Lanie, dear, is that you?" Granny asked.

"Yes, I'm sorry to be so rude, but I think figured it out. I know why Max was so upset. My ex showed up on my front porch, unannounced, Thursday evening.

He had flowers in his hand and when he said I owed it to him to go back to Michigan and marry him, I laughed in his face." Lanie heard herself ramble but couldn't stop until she explained the entire situation.

"Granny, Max must have seen this happen. It's the only thing I can think of where he may have gotten the wrong impression. I didn't accept the flowers and forced my ex to leave. He is the last person in the world I want to be with."

"Well, that's some story, Lanie. Can I ask you one thing?" Granny's calm voice comforted her.

"Of course." She held her breath.

"Who is the first person in the world you want to be with?"

Lanie exhaled. "Max. I want to be with Max." She

did her best to hold back the tears that formed in her eyes.

"Well, dear, I can say with confidence that your story holds water. I finally broke through that tough cowboy exterior and convinced Max to talk to me. He said that he saw you on the front porch with another man and that you must not want to be with him."

Lanie gasped.

"I told him he was wrong, dear. I see how you two look at each other and even if neither of you know it, yet the love in your eyes is unmistakable to me. Seen it a thousand times."

"Oh, Granny, what can I do to get through to him?" Lanie asked in a shaky voice.

Granny, always the matchmaker, knew what her grandson adored; she described to Lanie the one thing that Max couldn't resist.

TWELVE PADDED ENVELOPES sat in the front seat of Max's truck as he drove toward the USPS drop box in Bowie, each addressed to a different record producer in Nashville. Brad Daniels, Max's friend from when he played the bar scene, had given him advice when Max had planned to pursue his dream two years ago.

Max racked his brain to remember everything Brad had told him. However, his focus wasn't on the road in front of him. *How did I end up in front of Lanie's house?*

Her car was in the driveway; she was home. He could walk up to the front door and ask what he did to push her into the arms of another man. No. That's just asking for trouble. She's made up her mind.

With a final glance at the little house in Bowie, Max pursed his lips and said, "Goodbye, darlin'," before he shifted the truck into drive.

WHEN HE SAT down to dinner with Granny, she started the conversation as if it was any normal day. "How was your day, Max?" Granny squinted in his direction. His mind was somewhere else.

"Max, please talk to me. It's just the two of us tonight, your father is gone on that longhorn buy trip; you can tell me what's bothering you. You have never kept things bottled up for so long." From years of experience, Granny remained quiet and waited for Max to speak.

Focused on the potatoes on his plate, Max's voice came out low and steady, "I mailed CDs to Nashville." After he said the words, Max lifted his gaze to take in Granny's reaction, surprised to see her smile from ear to ear.

"Max!" Granny slid her chair out from under the table and stood to wrap her arms around her grandson's neck. "That is the best news I have heard in a month of Sundays. I am so tickled that you finally did it. Boy, you are going to be the next big country star. My grandson is going to be famous."

Max reveled in his grandmother's joy and stood to give her a proper hug. She squeezed so tight that he thought he would lose consciousness, but he knew better than to move away from Granny mid-hug.

A chuckle later, Granny released Max and held him at arms-length. "My boy, I'm so very proud of you. What does Lanie think about all this?" One eyebrow raised and Max understood that his grandmother knew more than she let on.

He answered with pursed lips, "She doesn't know."

9 LONGHORNS

"YOU GOT THIS." Lanie raised an eyebrow at her reflection in the rear-view mirror and convinced herself that the night she had planned would turn out to be fantastic. After one last swipe of pale pink lip-gloss, she was ready to claim her man.

Granny's voice repeated in Lanie's memory. "Max is usually finished with chores and out of the shower by seven o'clock. The timing would be perfect if you show up a little after that." Tips from Max's grandmother gave Lanie the perfect idea to prove to Max how wrong he was to assume someone else had taken his place.

Standing at the front screen door, Max whispered, "Damn" as he watched Lanie exit the Camaro. Her natural allure had been outdone by a white, off-the-shoulder sundress that clung to her thin frame and accentuated curves that Max found so sexy. Cowboy boots finished the look and made Max wonder if she had inside information on what he found irresistible.

Lanie's hair, pulled up into a messy ponytail, showed off her smooth, tan shoulders. Thoughts of his lips on her neck blocked out the rest of the world as he reached under the dress to lift it over her head.

"Well, Max." Granny's voice startled him and he cursed under his breath. She giggled and nudged her grandson out the front door. "Go talk to her."

A squeak and a thump from the screen door followed by Sam's panting accompanied Max's footsteps to the top step of the porch. "I don't think this is a good idea. She doesn't want me."

Max concentrated on every move Lanie made and frowned when she bent over to get something out of the passenger seat. *But, God, do I ever want her,* he thought and forced himself to look away as he tried to stop the sexy thoughts that ran through his mind. *I'm so screwed.*

Lanie carried a bottle of wine from the Markers Cellar Winery in one hand and a square tin in the other. "Hi, Max. It's great to see you." She tilted her head and smiled; a blush reached her cheeks.

The black cowboy hat covered most of Max's face and when he lifted his eyes to hers, Lanie thought she would lose her cool. Casual jeans and a crisp, white T-shirt were the embodiment of Lanie's concept of a cowboy. The only thing missing was an oversized belt buckle.

After a deep breath, Lanie pushed the tin toward Max. "I brought you something." Expecting the cold shoulder, Lanie didn't falter when he didn't react and instead shook the package. "Here, please."

Max couldn't stop the smirk that formed on his

lips when he opened the tin. "The way to a man's heart is through his stomach. How did you know that brownies are my favorite?" Max glanced over his shoulder at Granny and caught the wink intended for Lanie.

With a shrug, Lanie smiled and said, "A little birdie." She peered around Max and held up the bottle of wine. "I brought you something, too, Granny." When she reached beside Max, he caught the scent of vanilla as it radiated from her skin. It rattled him that her mere presence made his knees weak.

"Oh, my dear, you shouldn't have." Granny stood beside Max and accepted the gift. "Now you kids go have fun," she said as she closed the screen door.

"Max—" Lanie started to speak but Max interjected.

"Lanie, look, you didn't have to do this. I know you have another man. I'm not the kind of person to get between that. Besides, I told you, I don't share my women." He surprised himself with his steady voice. "But I'm glad you're here."

To keep himself from reaching out for Lanie, Max rested his hands on his hips. "That dress...you, um." Max sighed, "oh, God." He shook his head. "You look really great." If he didn't stare at the ground and watch the dust settle around his boots, he wouldn't be able to keep himself from kissing her. *That's not what either of us need.*

The warmth of Lanie's hand practically scorched the skin on his forearm. "Max, please, let me explain. Can we go somewhere and talk?" It troubled Lanie that he doubted what they felt for each other and she intended to set the record straight.

Sam trotted in front of them as he led the way through the barn to an old farm truck. Excited to ride in the bed of the truck Sam jumped in and barked, his tail wagged his entire body.

UNDER DIFFERENT CIRCUMSTANCES, Max planned to bring Lanie to this pasture full of long-horns to test her adventurous side. He thought back to her natural curiosity and knew this would be a fun area to start the tour of the Davis Family Ranch.

A longhorn approached and Lanie tensed at the sheer size of the gentle beast.

Max glanced at her and turned to hide his grin. She was in his territory; he was in control of the surroundings and their time together.

Lanie knew he would never do anything to put her in harm's way, so she convinced herself to stay calm.

"Look," Max faced Lanie and scowled, upset that he allowed himself to fall for her so soon after they met. "You could have told me you were seeing someone else before we made love."

"Max..." Lanie shook her head as she spoke.

"Please, let me say this." He raised his hand, palm out. "I stopped by your place the next evening to say a quick hello before heading home. I was so excited to get close to you, to think about a future with you. Then I saw you. You were standing on your front porch with a guy in a cowboy hat. He held an armful of roses."

"I know what you saw, Max. Or, rather, what you think you saw."

"You were laughing, for God's sake." Max scowled and lowered his head.

The scruff on his chin tickled Lanie's fingers as she coerced him to look at her. Wisps of her hair that had come loose during the ride to the middle of the pasture blew in the light breeze.

"I couldn't stop laughing because the idiot that stood on my front porch said I owed it to him to return to Michigan and be his wife." She snickered at the thought. "See, it's so ridiculous that I'm still laughing. How dare he tell me that I owe him anything after the way he treated me.

"What you didn't see, after I stopped laughing, was me slap him across the face when he tried to touch me." The thought of Ron's arrogance caused Lanie to frown and focus on the long grass beneath her feet.

"Did he hurt you?" Max whispered as he started to reach for Lanie, then retreated. Still unsure of what exactly had happened between them, Max hesitated to touch her.

"No, Max. He didn't." Lanie lifted her chin, her ponytail shook with the motion of her head. "I told him to get off my property and never come back. That I never wanted to see him again and I would never move back to Michigan. Then I went into the house and tried to call you."

A half step closer allowed Lanie to take in the scent of Irish Spring. She smiled and admitted, "I wanted nothing more than to tell my best friend about the strangest thing that happened."

"So...you...he..." Max shook his head, annoyed at how stupid he was, then searched Lanie's emerald eyes as he searched for the answers to their dilemma. After a sigh and a long pause, Max said, "I reckon I owe you an apology, darlin'."

Captured with each other's passion, they inched closer, both refusing to break the connection. Max's heart raced; he found the breath for a gruff whisper. "I'm sorry, Lanie. Real sor—"

Lanie trapped his words with a kiss.

Relief washed over Max like a wave. Elated that the distress of the last two days had been due to a giant misunderstanding, Max pushed his embarrassment to the side. No longer able to control his longing, he pulled Lanie as close as possible and held her so tight he fantasized about never letting her go.

"I have a confession, Lanie." Max's somber gaze spoke volumes. "I am relieved that you weren't with someone else. It broke my heart to think what I feel for you wasn't reciprocated."

Without taking his eyes off hers, Max leaned in for a brief kiss. "You have me wrapped around your little finger; you know that?"

A crooked smile formed on Max's lips and Lanie couldn't resist stealing another kiss. "Oh, do I?" She bit her lower lip and tilted her head.

Max let out a groan. "My god, you're so damn sexy. Without even trying, you're driving me crazy." Both of his hands framed Lanie's face as his mouth covered hers. When he pulled back to contemplate his next move, his eyes, black with passion, made her knees shake. Max ran his hands over Lanie's bare shoulders, down her back, to her hips.

Max's soft lips caressed Lanie's neck and she tilted her head back to allow her cowboy more access. He kissed a line from her collar bone to her shoulder.

"Max." Lanie pressed her body against his, longing to be intimate with him again.

"You are so beautiful, Lanie." He exhaled in her ear before he lifted her off the ground, sat her on the tailgate, and stood between her knees. "I can't keep my hands off you."

True to his word, Max allowed one hand to explore Lanie's curves while the other rested under her ear. He tilted her head to perfectly align their lips; their passion intensified.

Lanie ran her hands through Max's thick hair as he caressed her hip and moved his hand up her side. She moaned into his kiss and leaned into his hand as he cupped her breast.

Max broke the intense embrace and leaned his forehead against Lanie's as he struggled to catch his breath. "Jesus, darlin', you're killin' me."

"I love how you touch me, Max. Your lips, your hands." Lanie ran her hands across Max's muscled chest and down his six-pack abs before she unbuttoned and unzipped his jeans. "All of you." Her voice was husky as she scooted to the edge of the tailgate.

Surprised and delighted, Max's eyes widened along with his smile. "Lanie?"

She nodded and raised one eyebrow.

Eager to please his woman, he kissed Lanie with a

shared hunger while he completed the task of pushing his jeans to the ground.

"I WOULD BE happy sitting on the tailgate of this truck forever." Lanie rested her head on Max's shoulder and savored the peace that surrounded them; cattle walked past as they grazed and crickets chirped. Lanie felt like a character in a country song.

Max placed a kiss in Lanie's hair. "So, you and Granny did some scheming, huh?" Even though he couldn't see her face, Max knew Lanie smiled. "Uh, huh. That's what I thought. She gave you some pointers on how to get to me, didn't she?"

Lanie shrugged and Max released an honest laugh, then lowered his voice. "I love that you asked Granny for help. I love that you made me brownies. I just love so much about you, Lanie. Thank you for showing me how much you care about me."

Turning to face Max, Lanie held his gaze to express the depth of her affection. "I was heartbroken too, Max. To think I did something that caused you so much pain killed me inside. I never want to feel like that again."

Max smiled and placed a soft, lingering kiss on her lips.

"My feelings for you have grown so much and so fast, it's hard to grasp. I'm not used to falling for someone so easily; it's a little unnerving, to be honest," she admitted. Unable to stop once she started to profess her true feelings, Lanie continued. "But I have finally let myself admit that you mean the world to me, Max. Being in your arms feels so natural, like being home; I feel so safe with you."

Max beamed and kissed Lanie's nose. "Can we make a pact to never let something like this happen again? I promise to come to you if something doesn't seem right. We can work out whatever is on our mind."

"Yes. I promise the same." She nodded.

"So, I should probably tell you something," Max said with a sideways glance. "I mailed CDs to a few producers in Nashville." Unsure of how Lanie would react, Max steeled himself for her reaction.

"What?" Wide eyes accompanied a broad smile. "Oh my god, that's fantastic! I'm so excited for you. When will you hear back from them? How does breaking into the music industry even work?"

"Well, considering that I just mailed them yesterday, I have no idea." Shaking his head with disbelief that he actually took a step to follow his dream, Max continued, "they say a few months, but who knows. I made them a while back but decided not to send them because Dad is so focused on my taking over the farm."

Glancing away from Lanie, Max said, "When I thought there was no chance of being with you." Pressure from Lanie's hand on his shoulder made him pause, then focus on her face. "I figured, what the hell?"

"You looked so good on stage. And your voice." Lanie winked. "So sexy. So incredible; I love hearing you sing. But I must ask, was the song about me?" Lanie frowned, afraid that the truth might hurt.

Max nodded. "But that's kind of a good thing. Darlin', I have written more in the past two weeks, since we met than in the past year." A quick kiss expressed his appreciation. "You inspire me. You gave me a renewed confidence to follow my dream." He kissed her again, deeper than before. "Thank you, Lanie. I guess you're my muse."

She giggled and wrapped her arms around his neck, delighted to be so happy.

SHADES OF PINK and orange painted the sky and silhouetted longhorns grazed beyond the fence, next to the pond. "Do you ever tire of this view?" Lanie asked.

"Never. Every chance I get, I take a few minutes to enjoy the sunset. It baffles me that many, many years ago, my ancestors owned land as far as the eye could see. So many people lost everything during the depression and all their land became government property."

Lanie enjoyed the cadence of Max's voice and appreciated how he told stories about the past. About his family.

"Now, it seems like everyone and their brother is chunking off huge portions of land to developers that just want to make a buck. The strip malls and subdivisions popping up to the south of Bowie concern me. I pray every day that all the land around Sunset stays pure."

"Max..." Lanie started to speak and hoped that his feelings about her wouldn't change when she told him about the proposals she had been assigned at work, but they had been distracted by a streak in the sky.

"Did you see that? A shooting star." Max hopped off the tailgate and reached for Lanie's hand. "My mom used to tell me that when you see a shooting star, a loved one who has passed is showing their approval." With a wide grin and a twinkle in his eyes, Max looked to the heavens and whispered, "Thanks, Mom."

Once Max brought his attention back to Lanie, he wrapped her in a warm embrace.

"She approves of us." Lowering his head, he placed his lips to hers. A spark caused them both to chuckle and even with a brief interruption, the significance of the moment had not been lost.

10   DAVIS FAMILY FARM

ALL DAY AT WORK, Lanie smiled and happily completed tasks that had been mundane in the recent past. Max popped into her thoughts every time she turned her head; his eyes, his lips, his hands, his... *Yup, I'm hooked.*

Trace scents of Stetson cologne came in spurts as Lanie sat in her office. *How can I smell him? I didn't wear any of these clothes yesterday.*

Challenged with the most important project on her desk, Lanie tucked her hair behind her ear and forced herself to focus. The Davis property would most likely be a few hundred acres less in the next ninety days or so and the prospect bothered Lanie. She remembered how passionate Max had been when he talked about landowners selling off to developers.

She started to explain how her position had transformed after she accepted the job, but the shooting star stole their attention. The thought of explaining to Max that she had been assigned a design project of a three-hundred-acre development in Sunset made her stomach churn.

Maybe she would find the courage tomorrow after the deed was done. Better to ask for forgiveness than permission, right? Somehow the phrase didn't calm her nerves.

Calvin Fuller passed her office and barked, "Ten minutes, Lanie."

CALVIN FOLLOWED Lanie from the office in Wichita Falls to her house in Bowie and waited on the road for her to join him in the SAAB. Even though she had only known her co-worker for a few months, Lanie had an uneasy feeling about the man. She was thankful that they only had to share a car ride for a limited amount of time.

Signs for the Sunset exit arrived too fast for Lanie. Before she met Max, developing rural areas into pleasant places for people to live, shop, eat, play, even gather for church seemed like a natural progression. Now, it almost seemed unethical. A frown drew her eyebrows together and she twirled her hair.

Thoughts of potentially devastating effects flowed through Lanie's mind. *Max and his family must know everyone in this area; do they know the Davis family? Oh, God, what if they're friends and this is a huge debacle?* She heard a voice in the distance, but it didn't register that someone was speaking to her.

"Lanie!" Calvin's voice startled her. "You haven't heard a thing I said, have you? Where are you? I knew it was a mistake to bring a designer." He scowled at her across the cabin of his car. "I told Lance that just because you're attractive doesn't mean the old man will sell. He has this silly notion that old men love young curvy girls. Can you believe that he actually..."

"What?" Lanie interrupted and turned in her seat. "Did you seriously insinuate that I'm here because I'm pretty, not because I graduated in the top five of my class and I know my shit?" Heat radiated from her face; Lanie had never been so angered by someone's words.

Lanie struggled to control her breathing but had been determined to understand exactly what was happening. "So, Lance partnered me with you because I'm young and have a nice ass? That's great. I can't believe I fell for his praises."

"Calm down; stop acting like a child. God, grow up and start living in the real world. Sex sells. Old guys dig hot chicks." Oblivious to Lanie's reaction, Calvin continued. "Why do you think you got the job? Because you're smart?" Calvin let out a snort, then glanced at Lanie. "Oh, that's so cute. You did."

"WHY ARE WE TURNING HERE?" Lanie questioned Calvin's directions because the only property on this road belonged to Max's granny. She hadn't taken note of the address of the landowner on the plans, only the location of the development project she had planned.

Lanie didn't even know Granny's name. She assumed her last name was Walker, but that wouldn't make sense because she was Max's mother's mother. Oh, I'm so stupid. Stupid, stupid, stupid.

"Uh, Miss Top-Five-of-Her-Class, this is the Davis Family Farm. God, Lance was right, you really are a ditz." With an exaggerated eye roll, Calvin slowed the car and pulled into Granny's driveway.

Sweat started to bead at the nape of Lanie's neck and her heart rate accelerated. She let the derogatory comment fly over her head; Lanie had more important things to worry about than who didn't like her.

Possibilities of how she could stop this meeting raced through her mind. *Shit. What can I do? Can I say I left the files at work? No... they're in my lap. Can I fake an illness, or break my arm, or start screaming? I have to do something to make this stop before it starts. Max will never forgive me if he knows what I've been planning for his family's land. Oh, Dammit.*

"Earl Davis is the name of the person we're supposed to meet, today, right?"

"Uh, duh, genius," Calvin huffed and shook his head. His true colors proved to be a muddy brown.

Not letting on that she knew the family, Lanie nodded and allowed the condescension. Then it hit her; as if a thought bubble had appeared above her head, Lanie gasped. *Earl Davis, Granny's husband, passed away last year. Calvin wouldn't be able to convince anyone to sell off a portion of their land if that person was no longer alive.*

Max said something about a land trust and confusing legalese; that's why he didn't truly own the property on which he lived. Granny verbally gave him the land because her husband signed a hundred-year agreement that meant the land could not be split.

"Oh, thank God," Lanie whispered.

Fred Walker met the car in the driveway and, before Calvin had a chance to put it in Park, stood at the driver's side door. He hadn't noticed the person sitting in the passenger seat. Yet.

When the door opened, Fred addressed the unwelcome guest, "I only accepted to allow you on my property so I could tell you to your face that you're overstepping your bounds." Fred protected his family's land with a wide stance and hands on his hips. For an older man up against a young hot-shot sales rep, his persona demanded respect.

The patriarch of the family continued, "You need to leave. There will not be a meeting. I have been in touch with my lawyer and he assured me that there will not be any land sold. Your very presence is upsetting my family."

"You listen to me, old man." Calvin raised his voice and pushed toward Fred with unexpected energy. "I don't care what your lawyer has told you, this land will be split whether you like it or not. You just wait and see what kind of loopholes we can find in your so-called contract."

"What's all the ruckus out here?" Granny crossed the yard to stand beside her son-in-law. Sam jumped off the porch and barked as he raced to Fred's side. Lanie had never seen the dog so upset.

Fred tried to convince Granny to go back inside, but the stubborn woman refused.

It was only a matter of time before they discovered

another person in the car. Lanie had a hard time deciding if she should continue to hide or stand up for the people that had been so kind to her. Then she watched as Granny approach the men. *Don't be a coward. No one respects a coward. Granny needs me.*

Lanie refused to bear witness to anyone being treated like they didn't matter. Unable to wait any longer, she opened her door and stepped into the driveway.

"Calvin, stop it. Leave the man alone. Let's go." The strength in Lanie's voice surprised them both.

"Lanie?" Fred tilted his head and his lips parted.

She frowned and shook her head. "I didn't know. I'm sorry." To Calvin, she repeated, "Let's go. This meeting wasn't ever going to happen."

Calvin turned and glared at her. "Little missy, you need to mind your P's and Q's. This here is man's work." He turned back to Fred and continued, "The sooner you agree to our terms, the more money you'll get. If you try to hold out, Bauer & Bauer will ravish you. Trust me, it won't be pleasant."

"Lanie, dear, what are you doing with this wretched man?" Granny's disappointment crushed Lanie's heart.

"Granny, I didn't know—" Lanie didn't have time to explain before Calvin started to get aggressive.

"Y'all'd be better off if you just signed the paper-work today. I can assure you that here and now is the best deal you'll get." Papers shook in one hand while he held out a pen with the other. "Bauer &; Bauer is prepared to offer you $225,000 for the three hundred acres that border 101 and Lawhorn Rd. This offer is good for today only. Sign here."

"Son, you have lost your ever-lovin' mind. Hell no, I'm not signing that. I'm not signing anything. Ever. Besides, your offer is a joke. You really expect me to A: sell to a son of a bitch like you? And B: accept an offer of fifty percent less than the land's worth? You're not only stupid, but you're also bordering special."

Lanie approached Granny and shook her head. "I didn't know we were coming here. I didn't know they were trying to buy your land. I'm so sorry, Granny."

"I don't understand..." Granny winced and clutched her chest. "Fred..."

In slow motion, Lanie witnessed Fred reach Granny's side, put his arms around his mother-in-law, and support her weight as she sank to the ground.

Lanie grabbed her phone and dialed 911. She forgot that the cell service this far out of town was hit-or-miss, but she waited for a connection and prayed. *Please, God, let this call get through.*

Lanie placed the folder of paperwork under Granny's head to keep it out of the dirt. She knelt beside the older woman and thanked God for reception as she gave directions to the operator.

Fred's eyes turned black and he clenched his fists as he stepped toward the developer. It took every ounce of control to keep from punching the source of stress that caused Granny's collapse. "If anything happens to her, so help me God..."

Sam barked and Fred understood his fury. Fred grabbed the dog's collar just as he lunged at the wicked stranger.

Calvin didn't wait for Fred to finish his threat or for the dog to attack. He walked to the SAAB, opened the door, started the car, and backed down the driveway.

Dust followed Fred to the porch; in a flash, he returned with a pillow and blanket. "We can't move her until an ambulance arrives," he said to Lanie with a scowl.

"Mr. Walker, I'm so sorry. What can I do?"

"Call Max."

11 TEXAS SUMMER NIGHTS

SWEAT DRIPPED off Max's brow as he lifted the T-Post pounder again and again as he drove the post deep into the ground. He welcomed the release of frustration even if it meant sore muscles the next day. The chaos that had taken place at Granny's two days prior ran on a loop through Max's mind.

Lanie's panicked voice had come through the phone and Max raced to his truck. His thoughts turned to prayers focused on Granny's health. He realized the severity of the situation as an ambulance passed, having come from Granny's property. When he pulled into the driveway, Max found his dad waiting for him.

Reassured that Granny was in good hands and Lanie was with her, Max breathed for the first time in what felt like a month.

On the drive to Nocona Hospital in Bowie, Fred informed his son of the planned meeting with Bauer & Bauer and apologized that he hadn't told him about it sooner. Fred admitted how surprised he was to see Lanie with the buyer.

"What the hell was she trying to do?" Max raged. "Butter me up so I would convince my grandmother to sell land to the precious development company she works for? I'm such an idiot. I should have never let her back into my world."

"Now, son," Fred soothed, "Lanie had nothing to do with this. She was just an innocent bystander. She did everything she could to make that man leave."

Max didn't buy it. When he had time alone with Lanie, he pulled her into an empty waiting room.

Lanie spoke first, her face streaked with dried tears. "Thank God, Granny is going to be ok."

"No thanks to you!" Max erupted. "You did this. This is all your fault. My grandmother is in the hospital because all you care about is getting our land for that company you work for. Do you get a commission or something?"

"What? Max, please don't say that." Lanie gasped and shook her head.

"You were out scoping the area the day you—supposedly—almost run out of gas, weren't you?" Max accused, using finger quotes. "I know what you were up to. You never even told me what you really do for your job. How convenient. God, I should have known what you were up to when you begged me to take you back and practically threw yourself at me. Did you think having sex with me would automatically make me putty in your hands, so you could get your filthy paws on my family's land?" He couldn't prevent the glare in his eyes.

Caught off guard, Lanie exclaimed, "No, Max! I swear none of that is true. I—" Her words had been cut off by a wave of Max's hand. Depleted of energy, she lowered her head.

"None of that matters, now. Look," Max blinked away the memory of her smile. "You have to stop this. First thing in the morning, you're going to make your company stop pursuing this land. Granny can't handle any more stress. Her heart just can't take it."

"Max, this was not my fault. I did not do this to Granny. I think the world of her, you must know that by now. I'm so sorry; I truly had no idea that we were meeting with your family. I haven't told you exactly what my position entailed because I was focused on getting to know you."

"Mmm-hmm," Max pursed his lips and shook his head. "Don't try to talk your way out of this, *darlin'*." He almost spat out the last word.

Max had only used the term of endearment in a positive tone before. The thought of him being sarcastic with an expression she adored made her heart ache. "Please believe me. I didn't even know her last name was Davis. How could I? We hadn't even talked about that yet."

Max turned away from Lanie and gazed out the waiting room window.

She stood behind him for what seemed like an eternity. The thought of reaching for him came and went; she doubted there was any way to convince him to forgive her. A heavy sigh and footsteps indicated her retreat.

As she walked away, Max recalled the best days of

the past year. All because of Lanie. Drinking wine on the hilltop, Max began to appreciate Lanie as a truly beautiful person. Sitting on Lanie's back porch and later in her bedroom, he discovered her adventurous side. Talking and laughing in the pasture with the Longhorns, Max finally accepted his feelings for her.

Dammit, Lanie, I loved you.

MUSCLES SORE FROM HARD WORK, Max sat on the front porch and strummed his guitar. A slow melody he wrote for Lanie had him reminiscing. Fred came out of the house with two shot glasses in his hand. After he sat on the other side of a small table, he held out the whiskey for his son.

The burn from the drink stretched from Max's throat to his belly. Max shook his head, "Whoo. Thanks, Dad. I needed that."

"That's a new tune. What do you call it?" Fred had always been enamored with his son's talent, not that he had the courage to admit it.

Max chuckled, raised his eyebrows, and said, "*Texas Summer Nights.* It's not done. Just some random thoughts, at this point." Sam curled into a ball by his master's feet.

"Well, let's hear it."

Encouraged by his dad's nod, Max sighed and began to strum again. He lowered his head and closed his eyes. Lanie appeared in his daydream just before he started singing.

The slow rhythm and soft, even tone of his son's

voice lulled Fred and he closed his eyes so he could envision the story that Max told.

> We sit on a blanket under the stars
> every night
> Lanie kisses me and I pour her
> more wine
> She likes to feel my hands and the
> breeze in her hair
> Somebody pinch me, I must be
> dreaming
> I close my eyes and hold her tight
> Lanie's all I need on those Texas
> summer nights
> Last night I wished on a shooting star
> that the night would never end
> What I wouldn't do for just one more of
> those Texas summer nights

Fred masked a proud smile with a simple grin. "That's real nice, Max. Now, what are you going to do about Lanie? It's obvious you love her."

With a sigh, Max met his father's gaze and admitted, "Yeah, I guess I do. But..."

"Dammit, boy. Stop being so flippin' hard-headed. Lanie did not do this on purpose. What happened to your granny was not her fault. The doctors told us she would have had a heart attack soon enough, no matter what. Honestly, I thank God it was when we were around and able to help instead of..."

Fred's voice trailed off and he shook away the thought of losing Granny. "If you love her, go get her.

Don't let another misunderstanding keep you apart. I've seen how you look at each other. She's the one for you, Max."

"But..."

"But nothing," Fred leaned back in his chair and crossed a leg over his knee. "Listen. I want to tell you a little story. When your mom and I first met, we fell in love instantly."

Max hadn't heard a story about his mom in ages. He smiled and leaned forward. Sam's wet nose nudged Max's hand and he laughed. *It feels good to smile.*

"She was a barrel racer in the same rodeo that I was ridin'. Damn, she was a looker; long dark curls hung down her back and flew out to the side when she raced. It's a wonder that cowboy hat stayed on, she rode so fast. After the fourth or fifth rodeo, I got the courage up to ask her out. Back in those days, the girls could only hint that they liked you. It was a man's job to get his woman. I could hardly believe she wanted to be with a hoodlum like me."

Max sat quiet, mesmerized by the story and the cadence of his dad's voice.

"She said I was too late. She was riding in her last rodeo 'cause she was moving to Tulsa with her family. It took me a week before I realized that what I was feeling was love. My daddy told me that I better figure out a way to convince her that I was the one for her. When I found the courage to tell her how I felt, she was already gone. I was devastated."

"Well, what did you do?" Max asked.

Fred gazed over the yard, past the barn and the

longhorns to the tree on top of the hill. He chuckled. "I went and got her."

Orange and purple streaked the sky and Max sensed Lanie by his side; their connection was too strong to dismiss. "How could I be with someone that works for those kinds of people? She's designing for a developer, the one thing I don't want in my life. What can I do to get her?"

Fred smiled and nodded, "Hmm... I might just have the solution to that there conundrum."

12 FIREWORKS

PRINTED screenshots of the Davis Family Farm deed sat in Lanie's printer as she surfed the internet for more information. The tears dried up halfway through the night, along with the guilt of Granny's hospitalization. Lanie knew what happened wasn't her fault, but she had a desire to make things right.

Unable to sleep, the glow of the computer screen kept Lanie company. "Oh, thank you, baby Jesus. I knew there had to be a way to prevent Bauer & Bauer from buying that land." As she talked to herself, Lanie stood and stretched. Hours of research had paid off; now she could face Max and reassure him that nothing would change. At least not for the next ninety-nine years.

When Earl Davis found out he was sick, he found a way to protect the family farm. Developers had made numerous attempts at splitting his land for the sole purpose of building a residential area north of town, along TX-101—the same area Lanie designed.

AS LANIE SCOOPED tablespoons of coffee into the filter, a shrill ring startled her and grounds scattered across the counter top. *Shit. Who would be calling me at 7:00 am?* She picked up the receiver of her landline and said, "Hello?"

"Hello, dear. It's Granny."

"Oh, Granny. It's so good to hear your voice." Lanie sat at the table and forgot about the coffee. "Are you okay? How are you feeling? When do you get to go home? I'm so happy you called me. What can I do for you?"

"So many questions," Granny chuckled. "Let's see. I feel fine, I just now got home and settled on the couch. I thought about you all night; you must be so upset about what happened." After a pause to catch her breath, Granny continued, "Lanie. Please don't worry about me. The doctor said my heart attack was going to happen sooner or later and to be honest with you, I'm glad it's out of the way. Now I can continue living."

Breathing was the last thing on Lanie's mind and she almost forgot to do that too. Once she grasped that Granny was pretty much back to her old self, she released the pressure on her lungs. "I have been worried. I've been up all night."

"Listen, Lanie. I want to see you. Will you come over this morning?"

"I would love to, but..." Lanie hesitated, "but... Max..."

"Max needs to see you too. We all do,

dear." Granny paused. "Please, Lanie."

How could she possibly resist? Of course, Lanie would do anything to rectify the harm she believed she'd caused. In her mind, she—well, at least Bauer & Bauer and the work she had been assigned—was to blame for Granny's heart attack.

"All right. I'll be there around nine o'clock. Is that okay?"

"Perfect, dear. We'll see you then."

"SO, what I found in the deed is that..."

Granny waved her hand as if the words would be wasted breath. "Lanie, we are all aware of the details of the deed; that's the reason Fred was so stern with that horrible man. The contract is solid and we all know it."

With a tilt of her head and a sincere smile, Granny rested between sentences.

"You've done so much work, thank you so much for caring about our family to put so much time and effort into research. Please be assured it has not been time wasted; now you fully understand." Her thoughts turned to her grandson. "Max, why don't you and Lanie take some time alone to process all this information."

Max reached for Lanie's hand and offered a small if not sincere smile, but Lanie wavered. *Why is he was being so nice?* After a nod, she acquiesced.

In the late morning sunlight, the couple walked, hand in hand, through the barn, as they had only a few days before. Horse stalls and feed buckets sat empty, and a momma cat lay in the hay beside her five sleeping kittens.

Sam trotted beside Max as usual, and, as they exited the other barn doors, chickens scattered. Normalcy enveloped Lanie and she understood how life would exist on this farm.

"Lanie, I need to apologize." Max sighed, chuckling, and shook his head. "Again, it seems."

Electric blue eyes caused Lanie to sigh. Would she ever be able to resist that look? "Max—" she began.

"No, please let me do this." Max took both of Lanie's hands in his and began the speech he had practiced all night. "I should have asked about your work sooner. I should have thought through what it would mean to be with you...really be with you...after the passion and newness settled."

Max kissed the back of Lanie's hand, then took a step closer before he lowered his head and said, "I'm sorry, darlin'. So sorry for the mean things I said to cover the pain I felt for Granny. If I could take it all back, I would. I can't imagine how empty my world would be without you. Will you ever forgive me?" Max held his breath and waited patiently for a response.

"Oh, Max, of course, I forgive you. Granny is the most important person in your life and I understand how you would think it was my fault that she got hurt. I blame myself too." A single tear rolled down Lanie's cheek. "Please understand. I didn't know the land was yours." Tears filled her eyes. She blinked them back as she turned away from Max.

Lanie raised her eyes to the heavens and asked the

universe, *What am I going to do?* Unable to hold back any longer, Lanie covered her face with her hands as tears streamed down her face.

"Baby, please don't cry." When Max pulled her into a gentle embrace, Lanie released the anguish that plagued her. "Shh, darlin', it's going to be ok. I'm sorry. I'm here. We'll figure this out."

Lanie reached around Max's waist and held him close as if she needed his support to stand. Grateful that they were mere steps away from salvaging their relationship, the tears were more relief than sadness. It was still hard to believe she had fallen head over heels for this man so fast. Even though she'd tried to downplay what she felt, their attraction and passion had been undeniable from the day they met.

Max leaned back and confessed, "I want to be with you, Lanie." As he stared into her eyes and dried her tears, he spoke the words that he had been holding back. "Lanie Green." He brushed a stray strand of hair behind Lanie's ear, rested his palm on her cheek, and smiled. "I love you," he said without hesitation. He lowered his head, tilted it to the side, and waited for acceptance.

Lanie stared at Max and parted her lips but refrained from jumping into his arms and ravishing his face with kisses. She took a moment to grasp the meaning of his words. *Max loves me. He really and truly loves me. This is the real thing. Oh, my...*

Unable to wait any longer, Max pressed his lips to Lanie's and pulled her to him. She smiled under his kiss as he parted her lips.

Lanie welcomed his touch and reached around

Max's neck as she rejoiced in the reality that she loved a man that honestly loved her back. Following Max's lead, Lanie took a few steps backward until hay bales stopped her movement.

Her skin warmed under Max's touch and Lanie pressed her body against his. Their kisses deepened and passion grew until Lanie pulled away.

"Wait, Max..." His continuous kisses muffled her giggles. "Max," Lanie insisted and placed a hand on his chest to separate them. "I need to tell you something before anything else happens between us. It's important."

When Max took a step back and his brows formed a 'V,' Lanie almost felt guilty.

"Max?"

"What is it, Lanie?" Max's eyes searched hers. Concerned, he tilted his head and listened.

"Max Walker. I love you too."

"You little..." Max's crooked smile lit up his entire face. He lifted Lanie, sat her on the hay, and pressed against her. "You'll pay for that, darlin'."

"IT'S TOO bad Julia has a man in her life. I know someone who would really like her; she's just my friend Brad's type. They could make the perfect match." With the red plaid blanket and a basket in his hands, Max led the way to their tree on the hill.

"What type would that be?" Lanie strolled behind Max and giggled at Sam as he nipped at the corner of the blanket.

The couple shared the task of spreading the blanket over the tall grass and Lanie sat as Max poured her favorite wine from Marker Cellars into plastic cups. Sam stretched out along the bottom edge and sighed as he lowered his head.

Earlier in the day, Max and Lanie attended Julia's Fourth of July celebration and spent two hours smiling, laughing, and making new friends. Lanie brought her infamous cheesy potato casserole and the man she loved. It had been difficult to pin Julia down with all the guests but she made it a point to sit with Max and Lanie for a little while.

"You know, petite, blonde, pretty, smart, outgoing, a little sassy. Brad likes specific traits in a woman. I've told you about Brad, right?"

Minimal space separated the couple and Lanie felt heat from Max's shoulder. "You have. He's the drummer from your high school band, right? It's a shame you don't get to spend much time together." Lanie sipped the wine and leaned into Max, "Mmm. This is so good. Texas sunset in a glass."

"LANIE, why didn't you tell me about what you had been working on for Bauer & Bauer?"

Dusk enveloped the couple as the sun sank below the horizon. A chill found Lanie and she rubbed her bare arms. A blanket padded the ground as the couple sat under Max's mom's tree on the hill.

"I tried to, but"—Lanie put on her best puppy dog eyes—"you kissed me and I got lost in you."

"Fair enough." Max nodded and squeezed her shoulders.

"I don't know what to do, Max. I can't continue to work for this firm, but I moved my entire life and made decisions about my future based on my position at Bauer & Bauer." Lanie huffed, frustrated and disappointed.

"Even if that is a rhetorical question, I'm glad you asked." Max captured Lanie's attention. "My dad and I were talking and I think we may have a solution. I want to offer you a job on the ranch."

"Max, but..."

"Dad was right. If I get off the pot, I can start running the business like it's meant to be run. With the contacts I've made over the years and a little effort, I can easily double our yearly revenue. I want you to be my partner, Lanie."

Taken aback, Lanie's jaw dropped, drawing a chuckle from Max. "But...well...Max?"

"Think about it. We have a couple days before you have to go back to work. Let's just enjoy our time together and see how we feel in an hour."

"Max." Lanie poked his side and giggled. "Ok, let's think about it."

As fireworks illuminated the top of the hill, Lanie moved to sit in front of Max and leaned into his chest. He wrapped his arms around her shoulders and kissed her hair. "I love you, Lanie Green."

At the sound of Lanie's voice repeating the words, Max's shoulders relaxed and he closed his eyes. "Say it again, darlin'."

"I love you, too, Max Walker."

EPILOGUE

SEVEN MONTHS after sending tapes to a few producers, Max accepted an invitation for an audition in Nashville. He and Lanie made all the arrangements and planned to be away from the farm for at least a month. After Max signed a contract, his agent booked an introductory weekend show for two weeks later; he knew that the Texas native would rise to the top in no time.

"Texas Summer Nights" aired for the first time the following week and rose to number one on the local Nashville radio station immediately. It was the most requested song two weeks in a row before Max played his first professional show.

Almost one thousand people packed Blake Shelton's Ole Red bar on Broadway that night. Even though they stood shoulder to shoulder, future fans of Max Walker found a way to dance to the new, upbeat release.

The butterflies in Max's stomach disbursed a few

seconds after Max began to sing and the crowd surrounded the stage as if he were *someone*. Strumming the guitar as he sang lyrics written from his heart, he performed for the largest crowd of his life.

A blonde in the front row dressed in a tube top and a short, tight skirt began to dance as the song started. She blew a kiss to Max, licked her lips, and ran her hand through her hair. He shook his head, turned and pointed to Lanie, his passion for her clear on his face. Even the most beautiful fans could never compare to the woman he adored.

The drums reverberating through his body, Max stomped his foot and moved his shoulders to the beat as he sang.

> We sit on a blanket under the stars
>   every night
> Lanie kisses me and I pour her
>   more wine
> She likes to feel my hands and the
>   breeze in her hair
> I close my eyes and hold on tight
> When she moves closer, I feel my
>   temperature rise
> The sound of crickets and owls fills the
>   night
> Somebody pinch me, I must be
>   dreaming
> Life is so much sweeter with Lanie by
>   my side
> She's all I need on those Texas summer
>   nights

As sun sinks below the horizon and God
    paints the sky
The stars begin to align
Last night I wished on a shooting star
That this woman would never leave
    my side
What I wouldn't do for just one more of
    those Texas summer nights
She's all I need on those Texas summer
    nights

Louder than before, the crowd roared as the up-and-coming country star smiled and waved before walking off the stage toward the love of his life.

Lanie was waiting behind the curtain. The smile that spread across her face told a story of love and admiration. Her hair hung over one shoulder covering a portion of her lavender baby doll dress. With cowboy boots on, she stood almost as tall as Max.

"My Lanie!" He didn't care who was watching, Max lifted his muse off her feet and swung her in a circle before he wrapped her in his arms and kissed her. "I love you so much." This moment had been in his dreams for so long. Lanie's presence only elevated the experience past his expectations. Nothing could ever top this day.

"Max! You were absolutely fantastic! I'm so proud of you. You've done it—you made your dream come true. Congratulations. I love you." Lanie kissed her cowboy and hugged him tight.

"I'm only here because of you, darlin'."

THANK YOU FOR READING

Please consider leaving a review wherever you purchased, rented, or checked-out this book.

Reviews help readers find their new favorite stories!

LOOK OUT FOR

Texas Summer Nights Book 2

Coming Soon

ABOUT THE AUTHOR

KRISTI COPELAND is the author of contemporary and book club fiction. She lives in Texas with her husband and multiple critters on their ranch. When she's not writing, Kristi enjoys spending time with close friends, wine tasting, and cat collecting.

www.KristiCopelandWriter.com